UNRELENTING

World War II Trilogy, Book 1

Marion Kummerow

UNRELENTING, World War II Trilogy, Book 1

Marion Kummerow

This story is based on actual events. The main characters Q and Hilde have existed in real life under a different name. The author has tried to keep as close to real events as possible, but incidents, characters and timelines have been changed for dramatic purposes. Side characters may be composites, or entirely fictitious.

Marion's Newsletter

Sign up for my newsletter to receive exclusive background information and be the first one to know when Book 2 is released.

http://kummerow.info/newsletter

Table of Contents

Foreword

Dear Reader,

UNRELENTING is the first novel in my World War II Trilogy. It's a story dear to my heart, and I've wanted to write it for many years. But somehow I never found the time – or the courage – to look deep into the past and dig up the truth.

My grandparents Ingeborg and Hansheinrich Kummerow were two remarkable people I unfortunately didn't have the opportunity to meet, because they died long before I was born. But their story – one of courage and unrelenting spirit – intrigued me and captured me until I gave in to the overwhelming need to write it down.

UNRELENTING is for them, to remember their sacrifice and the difficult choices they – along with many others in war-ridden Europe – had to make. Research on World War II showed me how heroic even the slightest act of resistance was during those dark times, and my admiration for my grandparents, and all the brave persons in the German resistance, has grown beyond imagination.

From a prison cell, my grandfather wrote in one of his many letters…

"Ich lege durchaus Wert darauf, dass mein Andenken ehrenhaft ist."

"I want to be remembered honorably."

~Hansheinrich Kummerow

With this book, I hope to honor my grandfather's wish. Honor his and my grandmother's unrelenting spirit. Their love. Their legacy.

Sincerely,

Marion Kummerow

Chapter 1

Dr. Wilhelm Quedlin didn't know it, but today, the course of his life was about to change.

Q, as his family and friends called him, was on his way to work on this sunny October morning in 1932. Oranienburg was lovely this time of year, with trees flaming their fall colors along the banks of the Havel river.

Strolling through the gates of Auer-Gesellschaft, he quickly headed to his labs. Then stopped. The door to his office stood open, which was peculiar, but he entered nonetheless. He stopped just inside, surprise freezing him in his tracks. Two police officers were waiting for him. He recovered quickly and removed his hat, nodding to the men congenially as he placed it on the rack.

"Good day, gentlemen. What can I do for you?" he asked, trying to mask his surprise and worry with a polite welcome. An unexpected visit from the police was almost never a good thing. The political climate in Germany had grown increasingly tense, and everyone knew it was much better to keep a low profile these days.

"Doctor Quedlin, we need you to accompany us down to the police station," the older officer said, unashamedly eying Q with blank, dark eyes.

"Is there a problem?" Q asked, trying to remain calm even as his mind raced to identify anything he could have done wrong. And who might have been around to witness his error and report it. Telling on one's fellow man was no longer taboo like before, but actually encouraged by the government.

"You need to come with us now," the older officer repeated, stepping forward, his expression brooking no argument.

Q nodded and retrieved his hat from the rack he'd just hung it on. "Of course, officer." He stepped out of the office, keeping his eyes straight ahead and his hands in his pockets as he walked from the building, followed by the two police officers. On his way out, the eyes of his fellow workers watched him surreptitiously. Of course, they wanted to know what was going on, but without drawing attention to themselves, lest the police decided they too needed to be questioned.

The policemen ushered him from the building, past a seemingly perplexed gatekeeper and placed him in the back seat of a black DKW2. The motorized vehicle took off just as soon as everyone was inside. Q was squeezed between two officers, the seating very tight and uncomfortable from his point of view, but then again, the police were rarely concerned with anyone's comfort.

He looked straight ahead, seeing the people hurrying along the streets, turning their heads to avoid the passing police automobile.

No one seemed to even notice the beautiful sunny autumn day. Their minds were focused on getting to their destination and minding their own business. Even in his current predicament, or maybe because of it, he thought it sad that most people didn't share so much as a passing smile or warm greeting to the people they encountered along the street.

On their way to the police station, they passed the Oranienburg Palace, with its white stucco walls and red tiled roof as well as several brick and stone buildings housing churches and schools. As they approached the last intersection before the police station, Q noticed a small group of men wearing the SS *Schutzstaffel* uniform standing on the street corner.

Unlike the police officers currently riding in the vehicle with him, those men wore all black uniforms. Their caps were adorned with the *Totenkopf* skull and bones symbol, indicating they were loyal followers of the National Socialist German Worker's Party.

Nazis.

The late July elections had seen many parliament seats go to both the Nazis and the Communists, and political unrest was growing stronger with each passing day. Q sighed inwardly as he pondered on the reasons for the growing tensions.

With the crash of the United States Stock Market three years earlier, and the tremendous financial burden placed upon the German people by the Versailles Treaty to make reparations for Germany's actions in the Great War, the economy and people were suffering greatly.

Banks had collapsed, factories and entire industries were in jeopardy of closing, and people were ripe for some sort of change. This was evidenced when Adolf Hitler's Nazi party won an overwhelming thirty-seven percent of the popular vote in the most recent election.

Q looked at the younger police officer sitting next to him and asked, "Can you tell me what the problem is?" He understood very well that people didn't get taken to the police station for a minor transgression and wanted to know what he was facing.

"Doctor Quedlin, we–"

"Silence!" the older officer stated from the front seat. "He will find out soon enough."

Q bit his tongue so that he wouldn't make a pointed remark and incite the rude policeman any further. The trickle of fear he'd felt since seeing the police officers in his office had increased during the automobile ride. It now crept up his spine and made his neck hair stand on end.

Finally, the police vehicle stopped in front of the three story brick building, and he was ushered into the station that had most definitely seen better days. The wooden furniture was worn and very sparse.

Only two wooden chairs stood against the far wall, the only accommodations being made for visitors, of which Q was almost positive were few and far between.

The climate didn't allow for people to bring themselves to the police station unless the circumstances were dire and no other options existed.

He lowered his eyes and noticed the dirty and cracked tiles on the floor, which fit perfectly into the threatening and tense atmosphere of the entire place. Q's fear escalated, but he did his best to regulate his breathing and stay calm.

Do not let them sense your fear. You've done nothing wrong. Remember that.

But his self-talk did little to quell his nervousness when a ranking officer approached. "Doctor Quedlin?"

"Yes. Could someone please explain why I've been brought here?"

"Of course. Take him to the interrogation room," the ranking officer demanded, his voice harsh and intimidating. Another officer grabbed Q's elbow and led him down the hallway, pushing him into a sparsely furnished room featuring a large, bare bulb light hanging over a well-worn wooden table and three chairs.

"Sit!" the man barked, pushing on Q's shoulder until he took a seat.

The ranking officer entered the room and waited until the other one had left before he seated himself across from the table.

When the metal door snapped shut, Q felt a sudden surge of panic. He was trapped, and nobody could come to his rescue. The officer stared into Q's eyes, and Q tried not to fidget. "Oberkommissar Strobel," he said by way of introduction. "You know why you're here?"

"No, Herr Oberkommissar, if you would please let me know what this is about?" Q hoped the other man didn't hear the panic in his cracking voice.

Oberkommissar Strobel sent him a stern glance, "You are Dr. Wilhelm Quedlin?"

"Yes."

"What were you doing at Auer-Gesellschaft?"

Q took a deep breath. The police probably knew all of that already, but he would play their little game. "I work there as chief engineer in the chemical laboratory and supervise a team of scientists."

"Since when?"

"I started working for Auer-Gesellschaft four years ago after I received my PhD in chemical engineering from the Technical University of Berlin."

"What exactly did you work on?"

A puzzled look crossed Q's face. He had no intention of going into detail about his scientific research. After all, that was classified material. "Herr Oberkommissar, I wrote my dissertation about the thermal decay of nitrous oxide, and at Auer-Gesellschaft, this expertise served handy in researching and investigating new ways of finding a method to de-stabilize…"

Oberkommissar Strobel cut him off. "Enough." He paused for effect and added, "Doctor Quedlin, you have been accused of industrial espionage."

Chapter 2

Q looked at the police officer, letting the words register, and barely contained his laugh. *Industrial espionage? Me? That's ridiculous!*

He had collaborated with fellow scientists on many projects but stealing and selling that knowledge to someone else was not something he would ever do. No, he knew how hard it was and how much effort and dedication it cost to work in research. Never would his ethics allow him to even contemplate stealing the intellectual property of another scientist.

Oberkommissar Strobel apparently had some kind of evidence against him, and Q searched his brain to find something – anything – he could have done wrong but drew a blank. It would be best to wait until the Oberkommissar presented him with concrete accusations and compiled evidence.

That is, if he actually had any. It wasn't unheard of for the police to act upon rumors and accusations without any proof whatsoever. Just the hint of impropriety was enough to be punished these days.

He held the Oberkommissar's stare and said, "Industrial spying? Of what?"

The officer stood up, slammed his palms against the table and leaned forward until his breath wafted into Q's face. "What you have done constitutes high treason."

High treason? That was outright ridiculous. Q didn't

flinch and kept his voice calm. "Again, what evidence do you have to support those accusations?"

Q might be afraid, but he still was a scientist who dealt with cold facts and analysis on a daily basis, not with generalized assumptions. If the police didn't put facts on the table, they probably didn't have anything solid against him.

The officer looked at him. "Do you deny these accusations?"

For everything he knew, Q had a clean slate, and this knowledge gave him the strength not to succumb to the threatening atmosphere. He kept his poker face in place, looking into the officer's eyes. "You haven't actually made any. You've yet to tell me what exactly I have supposedly done wrong."

"How about working with the enemy?"

That's when it hit him, and Q had a sneaky suspicion that his only wrongdoing might be in his political opinions. Since the Russian October revolution when he was a teenager, Q had made no secret of the fact that he was rather fond of the ideas behind the Bolsheviks and Vladimir Lenin's idea of government. As a young and idealistic student, he applauded the actions of the peasants and working class who, in 1917, overthrew first the Tsarist autocracy of Russia and then the provisional government.

He still recalled the joy he'd felt on behalf of the Soviet people when the peasants and workers fought back against the punitive punishments and seized control of their government.

Communism seemed like the perfect ideology –

hand over the power to the people. Under that rule, there would be free and open elections, where representatives of the workers and peasants were elected to lead the country, rather than some autocratic monarchy ruling and serving only themselves. The idea that all people were created equal and that no one was worth more than anyone else agreed with Q's engrained sense of fairness.

Many of his compatriots felt the same way, believing communism was the only way to prevent war between nations and help the people live in peace with one another.

Q raised a brow in question. "Do you have evidence to support your accusation?"

Rather than respond, Oberkommissar Strobel turned on his heel and left the room without a word, slamming the door shut behind him. The sound of metal on metal caused Q to hunch his shoulders. He knew this was an attempt to make him nervous, and it worked, despite his best intentions to remain calm.

His mind wandered back to his time at university and how he had worked with a bunch of Russian scientists while doing the research for his PhD about the thermal decay of nitrous oxide.

"Q, your hypothesis seems plausible," Vladimir, one of the Russian master students, had stated.

Q had nodded. "By my calculations, the unwanted reaction of the nitrous oxide converting back to nitrogen gas can be minimized by reducing the amount of time the gaseous mixtures are in contact with the catalyst."

"That may be so, but what about the temperature as a controlling factor?"

Q had gone back to his lab and run some additional tests while the other scientists had done the same. Three weeks later, they'd made the breakthrough they'd been striving for. They were one step closer to manufacturing nitrates using industrial nitrogen fixation techniques.

The sound of steps passing the door to his room brought his mind back to the present. Was it possible that news of that collaboration was what had landed him in this interrogation room? He and the Russian researchers had shared many ideas, helping solve one another's glitches as they all strove to discover *the next big thing,* the one detail that would change the course of science forever.

They all wanted to leave a legacy in the world. To become part of history. Like Albert Einstein, a man Q admired immensely and who had received the Nobel Prize in Physics for his vast work in the field of theoretical physics.

Einstein was a professor at Humboldt University of Berlin and Q had been given the rare opportunity to sit in on several lectures where Einstein discussed his newly discovered photoelectric effect and the quantum theory.

Years later now, Q would always remember the privilege of listening to such a brilliant man and had striven to make his own marks upon science. Collaboration and the exchanging of research material was a part of that, and as long as the intellectual property being shared and exchanged was his, it wasn't illegal. At least not yet.

So what exactly did the police hold against him? What evidence could they possibly have to support their accusations of high treason and industrial espionage?

He decided it was best not to offer anything they might not already know about, but rather stand firm and make them produce the evidence. In these uncertain times, one never knew who was listening or what information might be interpreted incorrectly and out of context.

Accidently or on purpose.

Chapter 3

Before long, Oberkommissar Strobel returned to the interrogation room. "Tell us what we want to know."

Q shook his head, lifting his hands in question. "I've done nothing wrong. Tell me what it is I'm being accused of."

"Don't play dumb. You're an intelligent man if we can believe your biography. Trust me, this will all go better for you if you simply tell us the truth."

Q clasped his hands beneath the table to still their shaking. "I've done nothing."

Oberkommissar Strobel muttered a curse and once again left the room. Q sat there, his nervousness giving way to impatience as one hour became two and three. The more time that went by, the more worried he grew. His stomach growled and reminded him painfully it was already past lunch time, and he hadn't eaten in more than twelve hours.

They can't keep me here forever. They have to produce some evidence or let me go.

Just when he was about to knock on the door and demand to be released, the door opened again, and Oberkommissar Strobel entered the room with another policeman in tow.

The second officer held a piece of paper in his hands. Q recognized the paper; it was an article he had written about gas masks.

They must have searched my flat looking for evidence while I was detained here. That's why this is taking so long.

Q closed his eyes for a moment to keep the relief from showing in them. If the article was the only thing they had found to hold against him, he was off the hook.

The police officer put the article on the table, shoving it towards him. "Explain this."

Q forced himself to keep a straight face. This was not the moment for mirth or to give any indication of his sense of superiority. That would not go over well for him. No, he strove to appear daunted by the authorities, but cooperative and honest. A good citizen, willing to help the police.

"This is an article about gas masks. Where did you get this?" Q asked.

"In your flat. Amongst thousands of useless pieces of paper." The officer rolled his eyes and turned to his superior. "Herr Oberkommissar, his entire desk is covered knee-deep with notes, sheets of papers, magazines, and newspapers."

Q's mind formed the image of the carefully maintained disorder on his desk, and he groaned inwardly at the thought of how long it would take him to put everything back into its place. "For my research, I must collect all sorts of information and tend to retain every piece of paper I come across."

"That does not explain why you had this particular piece of paper, now does it?"

"No, sir. It doesn't because I didn't find that piece of paper. I wrote the article." Q pointed to his name on the upper right hand of the page. "See. That's me."

"Why did you write such an article?" the Oberkommissar demanded.

"Because I was asked to by my employer. I was tasked to research alternative and more economical ways of producing gas masks for the general population. To make them more affordable so all Germans could protect themselves. The article was published in Auer-Gesellschaft's technical magazine, which is printed on a regular basis. It provides an update on the progress and developments made by our research team."

The officers looked at each other, and Q felt the tension in the room easing. "So, your work was designed to keep Germans safe?"

Q nodded. "Yes."

"That is a very honorable and noble task. Were you successful?" the second officer asked, admiration now evident in his voice rather than accusation.

"Yes. I believe so. With so much talk about war and our enemies, my company wanted to give the German people a sense of security."

The officers both nodded. Since chemical warfare in the form of hazardous gases had first been used in the Great War, the general population had become almost manic about protecting themselves. With the general sense of hatred the German people felt from the rest of the world, owning a personal gas mask had become not only a recommended safety precaution but also all the rage.

The Oberkommissar gave him a smile, and Q nearly

sagged in his seat. "Wait here."

Both officers stepped outside the door, and Q listened to their muted conversation.

"Is that article all you found at his flat?"

"Yes."

"No evidence of spying activity or communication with our enemies?"

"None. We found no signs that he's particularly active with any political party."

"Well then, he can leave. Let him go, but remind him that he can't leave town as he's still under suspicion."

Q tried to act as if he'd not overheard their entire conversation when the second officer stepped back into the room. "Did you have more questions?"

"Not at this time. You're free to go, but you must remain in the district of Berlin until further notice. We will drive you home."

He could just imagine the face of his curious old landlady should he arrive home courtesy of a police car. He shook his head, stood up, and walked towards the door. "Thank you, but I prefer to walk."

The officer shrugged. "Very well. Your choice. Remember, don't leave town."

"I won't." Q left the police station and stepped back out into the now diminishing sunshine.

His flat was on the other side of town, and he found himself carefully observing the people he met as he embarked on the thirty-minute walk. He looked at every face, wondering what thoughts lurked behind their eyes. How did the police get suspicious? Had someone denounced him? And if so, who? Mentally, he examined each of his neighbors and colleagues, wondering who had snitched on him. Whom could he still trust? Anyone?

The answer was no one. He could no longer trust anyone.

Gloom was in the air, and Q believed Germany was on the verge of something major happening. The mood on the streets was restless, as if everyone was just waiting for the signal to act. Since the July elections, Hitler had been stirring the masses against the current government, and people were growing increasingly agitated. Q was hopeful that change for the better was coming soon, but today's events had him wondering.

He arrived at his apartment to find it torn apart, books and papers strewn everywhere. A deep sigh escaped him as he found emptied bookshelves, dumped out drawers and clothing scattered on the floor. Even his mattress had been tipped over in the police's futile search for compromising material.

Q held his breath before venturing into his small study, his *sacred space*. Here, nobody was allowed in out of fear of upsetting the fragile ordering system.

A pang hit him in the stomach, and he all but doubled over when he saw the devastation in his office. Every thematically sorted stack of paper had been turned upside down, and hundreds – no thousands – of pieces of paper lay scattered across the floor.

It'll take me weeks to organize everything in here.

Sighing, he returned to the bedroom and began to

put things back where they belonged. For the next few hours, he folded clothes and placed them back in the dresser drawers. He remade the bed and hung his business clothes in the closet.

The kitchen was next, and he was pleasantly surprised to find only one broken glass from the search. He tidied up the area and then headed for his study, where he gathered up the piles of paper filled with formulas, sketches, and calculations into several big boxes. He replaced the books on the shelves and arranged the chemistry magazines back into a pile.

Once he was satisfied that the room at least looked tidy again, he opened the hall closet and used a bread knife to pry loose the floorboard at the back. He took out a handful of *Reichsmark* notes.

His breath whooshed out of him, and he pressed his hand to his forehead. Thank God. They hadn't discovered the hidey hole where he'd stashed money, not completely trusting banks since their collapse a few years back. Each week, he added a few more marks to his stash. He didn't know what he was saving it for, but he knew there would come a day when it would not only be welcome but necessary for his survival. He wanted to be prepared.

Chapter 4

Hilde Dremmer glanced at her watch and groaned. *Two hours left.* Today had been a boring and tedious workday at the insurance company where she processed insurance claims.

She got up and walked over to the small kitchen, smiling at two of her friends and colleagues, who were brewing coffee and making plans for the upcoming weekend.

"Hey, Hilde. Are you sure you won't join us?" Erika, a pretty, curvy brunette asked, a pleading note in her voice and a pout upon her lips.

Hilde wrinkled her nose. "I moved to Berlin to have fun, not attend some boring political discussion."

"It won't be boring," Gertrud promised with a nod that made her ponytail hop up and down. Gertrud was the proverbial German girl with her sandy hair, blue eyes, and healthy pink cheeks. While Hilde herself had blue eyes, her hair was darker; long light brown strands she usually wore in a bun.

"So you say. I really have no interest in politics," Hilde answered. Her father had planted that seed in her head as a young girl, and it had stayed.

Politics are not for women, and you'd be wise to remember that. Keep your hands as far away from politics as you can, and you'll do fine.

"Don't you want to know what people are saying?"

Erika asked, cocking her head to the side.

"Not really. There are more fun things to do for twenty-year olds like us, don't you think? Let's go to the movies instead."

"We went to the movies last weekend, remember?" Gertrud reminded her, then wiggled her eyebrows up and down. "We might meet some cute guys at the debate," she added, as if that was reason enough to be bored for hours.

"Some of the politicians are really handsome," Erika said, a pleading look on her face.

"Handsome? Like who?" Hilde asked, her interest mildly piqued.

Her friends shared a look before Erika answered, "Like Adolf Hitler and some of his party members."

She had heard the name before. "Isn't he that politician with the National Socialist German Worker's Party?"

"Yes, the Nazis," Gertrud said. "And you really should come listen to him. He has so many great plans for Germany."

"And he's handsome," Erika added.

Hilde snorted, recalling a picture she'd seen of him in the local newspaper. "He's so not my type. And that ridiculous mustache of his. Come on, girls, you can do better than him."

She didn't add that she'd read about some of Hitler's ideas and was appalled by his ideas about racism. How could one even think about penalizing someone because of his or her race or ethnicity? Shouldn't every person have the chance to be acknowledged for her character and not for her ancestors?

Changing the subject, she asked, "There's so many fun and exciting things to do here, not like that boring suburb of Hamburg where I grew up. Why don't we go out and have fun?"

"There's a new movie playing. We could go see that," Gertrud offered as an alternative.

"Sounds good," Hilde agreed, warming to the idea. "And we can go to a dance afterward?"

"I'd love to," Erika agreed, worrying her bottom lip. "I guess I can hear Hitler speak another time, but I'll have to make sure it's okay with my parents first."

Hilde was torn between relief and sadness as she thought about her friends needing permission. She no longer had to deal with her overprotective father and step-mother. She'd left them behind, along with her two half-sisters when she'd come to Berlin to live with her mother two years ago. Her mother, Marianne "Annie" Klein, cared little for what her daughter did or how long she stayed out each night. She never asked about Hilde's friends, where she was going, or what she would do once she got there.

"Do that tonight," Hilde suggested.

"I will."

"If they don't agree, we could always find something else to do. There's so much going on here in Berlin. Culture and concerts, and museums…"

Erika and Gertrud shook their heads, "Yes, but it's not like it used to be," Gertrud said, pitching her voice low. "Everything was a lot more carefree years ago, but now it seems everyone is so tense. Almost depressed." She lowered her voice further. "And there are police everywhere."

"My father says Berlin is filling up with bad people," Erika added, keeping her voice low too. "Everyone has to watch everyone else."

Gertrud nodded. "I can remember when the idea of a political meeting was unheard of. Now, there's a meeting of some sort almost every night."

"That's because people are scared. No jobs. No money. And the democratic parties currently in power don't seem to be helping." Erika's voice was just above a whisper. "The Nazis and the Communists are the ones bringing us hope. A new government that's not afraid to speak out for our nation and willing to turn the economy around."

The three women sipped their coffee, growing quiet as they reflected upon the changes Germany had already seen in the last year. The government had changed leadership twice now, yet unemployment was still on the rise, with a staggering six million people or thirty percent without a job. As a result, poverty could be seen everywhere, and even those employed had difficulties making ends meet in this declining economy.

"Well, enough of this depressing talk. I need to get back to work and so do you two," Hilde said. They grinned and returned to their desks. Hilde had no desire to join the ever-growing army of the jobless, desperate people they'd just been discussing and got back to processing the claim in front of her.

Chapter 5

The next morning, Q arrived at his office, rested and in a good mood, considering how poorly his day had gone yesterday. He had a smile on his face as he approached the gatekeeper and gave the man a small wave.

"Good morning, Herr Schmidt."

The guard looked perplexed for a moment and then his face turned sad. "Doctor Quedlin. I'm afraid I can't let you inside the building. I've been instructed to escort you to the director's office should you turn up."

His smile fell. "What are you talking about?" Panic gripped him as dread crept up his spine.

"I'm very sorry, Doctor Quedlin. I don't have a choice in the matter." The poor man wasn't able to meet Q's eyes. "I've always liked you, sir, and I can't tell you how much it has meant to me that you always treated me like a valued person."

Most of the scientists looked down upon anyone less educated. Q felt ashamed for the way his colleagues treated the guard like a non-person. "You are a valued person, Herr Schmidt, and never forget that. Any idea what the director wants to see me about?"

The guard shook his head. "No, but I was instructed to take you directly to his office if you arrived or lose my job."

Q raised a brow. "Well, I wouldn't want you getting

into trouble on my account." He allowed the guard time to lock up the guard shack and then walked beside the man as they headed for the director's office, located in the administration building. On the way, they didn't talk, and Q wondered what had happened. After the police let him go yesterday, he was sure everything was okay.

As they entered the administration office, he passed numerous co-workers. Not one of them would greet him or meet his eyes. They all looked the other way or pretended to be too busy doing something else to notice him. So everyone knew he'd been accused of industrial espionage.

The behavior of his co-workers stabbed his heart. He'd been working at Auer-Gesellschaft for four years now and been promoted to chief engineer three years ago. And while he wasn't a close friend with anyone at work, he'd considered them good colleagues. He hadn't done anything wrong, and yet everyone apparently judged him on the mere accusation and shunned him.

Herr Schmidt stopped outside Director Hoffmann's office and tapped on the door. "Doctor Quedlin has arrived."

"Thank you. Send him in and wait outside."

Q didn't like the sound of that but entered the office anyway. He and Director Hoffmann had never been the close friends the rumors about his quick promotion alluded to, but they shared a mutual respect for one another.

"You asked to see me, Director Hoffmann?"

"Doctor Quedlin, I'm going to get right to the point."

The director had never been a man of many words, and today was no different. Yet, Q sensed there was an underlying fear to his brusque words. "Effective immediately, you are no longer employed with Auer-Gesellschaft. The gatekeeper will escort you to your office where you can retrieve your personal effects. Your notebooks and research belong to the company, and they are not to leave the premises. You will then leave and not return."

Q's heartbeat thumped in his ears. "Sir, I don't understand. If this is about yesterday, the police let me go after realizing they had made a mistake." Q couldn't believe the words of his superior. His work was his passion and he was about to lose everything, because of…what? A false accusation?

Director Hoffmann looked torn but stuck with his decision. "I cannot risk my own career and well-standing with the authorities by continuing to employ men who have been accused of espionage."

"But the accusations are false. They searched my apartment and found nothing. I have never done anything wrong!" Q raised his voice, trying to get some sense into the man who was about to fire him on a whim. "You should know that I'd never steal from my co-workers or our company. Haven't I proven time and again in the last four years that I always have the best of Auer-Gesellschaft in my mind?"

"That may be, but the suspicion has been cast, and I cannot have myself or this company under suspicion as well." Director Hoffmann turned around, effectively dismissing Q.

"There is nothing I can say to change your mind?" Q asked in one final attempt to salvage his job.

"No. I'm sorry."

Q shrugged and stepped out of the office, looking at Herr Schmidt. "Let's go. I'm fired."

The gatekeeper looked at the ground and shuffled his feet, murmuring some unintelligible words. They made their way back to the laboratory building and Q's now ex-office. His mind worked overtime as he acknowledged he was simply a victim of the fear that seemed to drive everyone these days. Fear of losing their jobs. Fear of being under suspicion. Fear of the police. *Fear of being alive*, he thought bitterly.

He didn't blame the director for making sure his notebooks stayed in the lab. As things had become more politically tense in Germany, the government had started classifying all research. In fact, his work had been considered so critical to national defense in the case of an upcoming war, he'd been forced to sign a non-disclosure agreement. Which he'd adhered to. So much so, that he hadn't even mentioned it or his work to the police yesterday while being interrogated.

He took one final look around, to the desk and worktable where he'd done some of his best work the last few years, then glanced through the window to the adjacent lab. Sadness swept through him at his loss. He would no longer have access to the research equipment and fruitful cooperation he and his colleagues had shared.

He turned away, focusing his attention back on the framed picture of his mother, Ingrid, and a coffee mug she'd given him for his birthday. He opened his briefcase and placed both items inside.

As his glance fell to an open notebook on his desk that featured the same chaotic order as his desk at home, he traced a finger over the formulas on the open page, his heart growing weary.

For the last several months, Q had been working tirelessly on new methods to analyze organic arsenic compounds. While methods for detecting other chemical weapons, including chlorine, phosgene, and mustard gas were in existence, none had been fully developed to detect arsenic compounds.

Prior to the Royal Air Force of Great Britain intervening in the Russian Civil War in 1919, the detection method had been unnecessary. Not anymore. The chemical lewisite, an organic arsenic compound, was not only a lung irritant but also a vesicant, causing blisters to form on those exposed to it.

Since the compound was both odorless and colorless, the only indication of exposure occurred when it was already too late, and those affected began to feel the stinging pain on their skin, in their respiratory tract, or in their eyes. Being able to detect this potential chemical weapon was a critical improvement in the defense of Germans against chemical warfare.

Q had been on the verge of making a breakthrough discovery, but now it would be up to his co-workers to find the last piece of the puzzle. One of them stepped into the lab and Q reached for one of his notebooks. He just had to make sure his latest discoveries wouldn't be forgotten.

He turned to the gatekeeper. "Just let me give my notes to my colleague and I'll be ready to leave."

Herr Schmidt looked slightly hesitant about allowing this, but before he could say a word, Q sauntered into the lab. "Arnold, my latest notes are in there. They'll be helpful in finding the detection method."

His colleague jumped at the words, apparently not aware that Q had entered the lab. "I...you...thanks." He took the notebook in a hurry and appeared to want to back out of the laboratory. Q's heart broke a little bit more. Why did everyone treat him like a leper?

"Wait. I believe we've ruled out the possibility of using water as the method of detection. While using a pH indicator to detect the formation of hydrochloric acid is plausible, the resulting secondary reaction is only slightly less dangerous."

"I have to go."

Q's shoulders sagged as he watched the man he'd so closely work with for years flee as if retreating from a monster. Dejected, he returned to his office and left, not allowing himself to look back as Herr Schmidt escorted him to the front gate. There he shook the guard's hand. "Thank you."

"Doctor Quedlin, I'm so sorry this is happening to you."

"Take care," Q said and headed off down the street. Since all his personal belongings had fit inside his briefcase, he didn't bother to go home. He would enjoy the unexpected day off, he decided, maybe visit a café. He took the suburban train, to Berlin Friedrichstrasse, and from there made his way to the main thoroughfare where people liked to congregate and socialize, Unter den Linden.

He chose a vacant table at a small café and ordered a coffee while he contemplated his next move. Many people passed by on this morning in October, a few very well off society ladies, but also a large number of poor people. Beggars. Most of them coming and going to one of the labor bureaus in the hope of securing some sort of meager employment, even if just for this one day.

The longer he sat there, the angrier he became. *First, I'm accused of a crime I haven't committed, and then I'm fired for the same crime I haven't committed. What kind of world am I living in? Since when is an accusation all it takes to stigmatize a person?*

Q was a scientist right to his bone, always had been. He throve on facts. Numbers. Formulas. But there were no facts involved at his layoff. Just empty accusations and fear. He brought the cup to his lips, inhaling the sweet yet bitter aroma of his coffee before he took another sip. The hot liquid filled his mouth, bringing a sense of warmth and comfort.

It was time to stop commiserating and start analyzing his options. To be truthful, he hadn't been happy at his job for quite some time. Not since his work had been classified as "important to the war." Maybe Director Hoffmann had done him a favor by firing him? At least now he was free to pursue his true passion – inventions for the good of humanity, not to the service of a government preparing to go to war.

War was horrible. He'd been a teenager during the last war, too young to understand, but old enough to wear the scars on his soul. He hated what it did to people and the destruction it left behind. He hated what the mere threat of another war was doing to people now. And he hated the capriciousness that seemed to rule the decisions nowadays. Like getting fired on an untenable accusation.

Still, he couldn't get rid of the nagging gut feeling that things in Germany were going to become much worse.

Chapter 6

One week after his first visit to the police station, Q awoke to a pounding on his door and voices demanding he open it up.

He scrubbed the sleep from his eyes and opened the door to see the same policemen standing there. "Doctor Quedlin, you must come with us now."

"What's this about? We've already been–"

"Now." They stepped forward as if to grab him.

Still sleepy, he said, "Let me get dressed and put on shoes first."

"Very well. Make it quick," the older officer said.

Q nodded and retreated to his bedroom, where he quickly donned his clothing and his shoes. He also grabbed a jacket as the weather had turned cold and blustery, and November mornings could be very chilly.

"Come along," one of the officers said, turning to leave.

Q followed them to the waiting black DKW2 police car and then into the station where he didn't believe his eyes. Klara Haller, a former colleague, paced the hallway, taking quick puffs on her cigarette. Her pacing increased when she saw him, but she butted out her cigarette in an ashtray and followed course as the two policemen ushered him into the interrogation room.

Still without a clue as to why she was here, or why

he was here for that matter, he took a calming breath and decided to wait and listen.

"Why haven't you arrested him? He's a dissenter and a traitor," Klara said in a high-pitched voice.

"*Fräulein*, if you could just–"

"This man has been working against the German government and must be stopped."

"Please stick to the facts. Now, would you please tell Doctor Quedlin what you told us?"

Klara struggled to get control of her emotions, then gave Q a scathing look. "He's been talking about Russia and how perfect the ideas of communism are."

"You've heard him say such things?"

She nodded. "He spoke of some Russians he once worked with."

"When was this?" the older officer asked, making notes on the paper in front of him.

"I don't remember," she said, lifting her chin.

"Did you see him talking to these Russians?"

"Well...no, but he likes the idea of communism. Ask him." She pointed a finger at Q.

The officers turned their attention to Q, the older one asking, "Is Fräulein Haller correct? Do you sympathize with the Communist Party?"

Being a member of the communist party wasn't illegal, but in the opinions of these police officers, it was apparently akin to being an industrial spy. Q shook his head and carefully chose his words. "I'm a scientist, not a politician. I've never engaged in any sort of political activity, not even while I was at university."

"So you deny being a Communist?"

"Don't you think inventions and progress should benefit all people? Not just a few rich elite factions?" Q faked a calmness he didn't feel.

"What's he talking about?" Klara demanded to know.

Q had seen the flicker of doubt in the eyes of the policemen and knew he could win them over if he tailored his arguments to agree with their mindset, even if only in part. He decided to appeal to their sense of justice, but even more so to their need of safety for themselves and their families.

"Remember that article you found in my apartment last week?" He waited until the police officers nodded. "That gas mask was intended to be affordable to everyone. Wouldn't it be better if any citizen, including the police and their families, had a gas mask available to them and not just military, high ranking government officials, and rich people? Wouldn't you feel better knowing your families were protected while you were at work?"

Klara glared as the police officers nodded, accepting Q's argument, and she interrupted with a high-pitched voice. "Don't let him fool you. He has connections to the Communist Party."

The officers looked torn for a moment. The Communist Party was not something anyone readily admitted to, not when faced with the local authorities. They were seen as radicals and troublemakers.

"Fräulein Haller, do you have proof of these

associations?" the younger policeman asked, and Q mentally congratulated himself. Finally, the discussion steered back on grounds based on *hard facts*, not nebulous suspicions.

Klara looked uncertain for a moment and then shook her head. "No."

Confidence surged in Q, and he instinctively puffed out his chest. "I think my colleague may have misunderstood some of my comments. I may have mentioned Russia in a conversation about some new advancement or invention that had been brought to my attention, but no more so than I have mentioned America or England."

The older officer looked at Klara. "Is that true?"

She scowled at Q and slowly nodded, "I guess. But he belongs–"

The officer held up his hand. "Doctor Quedlin, which political party do you belong to?"

Q shook his head. "None of them. I've never joined a political party."

The police officers had reached their level of tolerance for Klara's accusations. "Fräulein Haller, it seems you have no facts to back up your claims that Doctor Quedlin is a sympathizer with the Communists."

Then he turned toward Q and asked, "Doctor Quedlin, under what context would you have discussed America or England?"

Q smiled as a wave of relief coursed through his veins. "Four years ago, in the final stages of finishing my PhD thesis, I was privileged to spend six weeks visiting England. While I took some time for vacation, I was also allowed to attend a scientific conference in the field of organic chemistry. The attendees were renowned scientists from many countries, but I especially liked the British and American colleagues. They have some of the most advanced methodologies in the world, and it was a pleasure to exchange new approaches to research and minor breakthroughs with them."

"So you returned home after six weeks?"

"No, officer. I was also privileged to attend the 1928 Summer Olympics in Amsterdam while travelling, where I cheered for the German athletes to win medals for our Fatherland. In fact, I witnessed Ingrid Mayer win the female floret, and Georg Lammers gain the bronze medal in the 100-meter sprints. Both were sublime moments of national pride. If you wish to see my official accreditation, I can present it to you later today."

The officers shook their heads. "That won't be necessary."

The younger officer spoke up. "Doctor Quedlin, can you explain why one of your colleagues had reported you saying, and I quote, 'Everything that has to do with the Nazis is ridiculous.' It was also reported that, on more than one occasion, you made fun of them."

Q frowned, and a queasy feeling settled in his stomach, the conversation was steering into dangerous territory. He made a mental note to be more careful in the future and never openly ridicule the Nazis again. Apparently, in these days, it was better to duck his head and keep his mouth shut – just like everyone else.

Thinking feverishly, he once again stated, "I may have said this, trying to be funny. Apparently it wasn't a good joke. And what do I know of politics? I'm a scientist. Everyone in this room," he looked from one officer to the other, before he continued, "is surely better prepared to judge whether the Nazis are a veritable party or not."

His heart beat in his throat, and he prayed they wouldn't delve deeper into the Nazi issue. This might have the potential to get him into serious trouble.

Thankfully, the police officers seemed to get tired of the fruitless conversation. "Fräulein Haller, this man is no threat to the German Nation or a Communist Party sympathizer. Be more careful in your accusations from now on." The officer gave her a warning glare before turning to Q. "You're free to go."

On the way back to the exit, the policeman lowered his voice and spoke to Q. "This gas mask you've been working on? Is it already being sold?"

Q had to swallow down a chuckle and answered in the most serious voice he was capable of. "Officer, Auer-Gesellschaft has not put it on the market yet, and unfortunately, I was released from the company after the interrogation last week."

When he saw the man's disappointed face, he was reminded that policemen were only fellow humans following their orders. Since they hadn't been rough or mean with him, he added, "I believe if you ask Director Hoffmann for a prototype of the gas mask to conclude your investigation, you'll receive one."

He bid his goodbyes and followed Klara Haller from the building. Once out on the street, he grabbed her arm and turned her to face him. "Why did you do that?"

Klara gave him a disbelieving look, pulling her arm from his grasp. "You of all people should know!"

Puzzled, he observed her for a moment and then shook his head. "So, this is your revenge? To get me arrested for high treason?"

He felt his voice rise and strove for calm. Klara had fallen for him since she joined the company a year ago and had pursued him relentlessly. She was a beautiful woman, but nothing about her attracted him. So he'd turned her down many times, declining her dinner invitations, movie invites, and requests to be his date at company socials.

She shuffled awkwardly and mumbled, "I was just doing my civilian duty to keep my eyes open."

He shook his head and left her standing without a further word. Women like her were one of the reasons he was still a bachelor at the age of twenty-nine. That and the fact that he just hadn't met a woman he was interested in. His first love was science and women were only a distraction. No woman alive would appreciate him spending yet another night in his lab because he was so close to finding the missing link. He could do without the headaches having a girlfriend brought with it.

Q walked down the sidewalk, pondering on the economic and political climate in Germany. *Things are going to get a lot worse.* His country was in trouble, and if something didn't change, it was headed directly into doom.

On the walk home, a growing urgency to do something arose in his mind. But he couldn't even begin to fathom what that would be. What could a single scientist do to save his country from war and destruction? To save it from itself?

Chapter 7

Hilde and her girlfriends entered the theater foyer. Thanks to Hilde's step-father, Robert Klein, they'd secured tickets for the highly coveted opening night of the opera *The Marriage of Figaro* by Wolfgang Amadeus Mozart. They patiently waited their turn at the concession counter, wanting to purchase a soda before the performance began.

"Look at those guys over there," Erika pointed out in a whisper.

Gertrud and Hilde dutifully turned their heads. "Where?"

"The guys, lounging against the wall."

The three girls looked at the men, and Gertrud mused, "They look like they're seated in one of the private theater boxes." Even before she'd finished speaking, three women, dressed in the latest fashion gowns and adorned with expensive jewelry exited the bathroom and looped their arms with the guys.

"Look at their clothes." Gertrud sighed. "I'd love to be able to dress like that."

"Why don't you?" Hilde asked.

Gertrud looked at her long, mid-calf length navy blue skirt and sighed. "Apart from not being able to afford a designer gown, my mother would kill me before allowing me to leave the house showing even a tiny bit of cleavage."

Erika nodded. "My parents would dress me in a sack if they could." She pointed to where her skirt ended and her nylon stockings began. "My father doesn't like men being able to see my ankles. He says it's not ladylike."

Hilde laughed and glanced down at her own clothing. An elegant yet comfortable and warm pants suit. "You girls and your nylons. I don't know why you insist on wearing them during winter. You're always getting runs in them and going to the seamstress to get them repaired."

"That's because they're expensive."

"And cold. Not only do I not have to spend my money on getting my nylons fixed, but my legs stay warm. It's much more practical in this weather."

Berlin in November could get frigid, and this evening was a perfect example. The air temperature was near freezing, and while no snow had fallen yet, the potential was strong given the clouds that had been gathering all day.

"My mother would never allow it," Erika said, pouting. "Pants are for men, she insists."

That comment stabbed at Hilde's heart. Sure, she loved wearing pant suits in winter, but she didn't love her own mother's lack of caring. As far as her mother was concerned, Hilde could leave the house stark naked and she wouldn't object.

"Hey, those guys are awfully cute." Erika nudged Hilde's arm.

Hilde turned her head and made a face. "Those are boys, not men."

"What are you talking about, Hilde?"

"They're way too young and immature."

"They're about our ages," Gertrud said.

"Precisely. Too young." Hilde turned to enter the movie theater.

Erika giggled and asked, "So what are you looking for in a man?"

Hilde thought for a moment and then ticked the list off on her fingers. "Well, for starters, he should be older and more mature than me. He should be self-confident enough to love me just the way I am. And most importantly, he should be willing to stick around and not leave me at the first hint of trouble."

Where did that come from? Hilde was surprised at her own words. Why did she instantly assume someone would leave her?

"Is that all you're looking for?" Erika teased.

Hilde shook her head. "No. He has to have strong principles. He needs to believe in what he does and be willing to stand up for it. I don't want a man who bends at the first sign of adversity."

Gertrude rolled her eyes and Erika giggled.

Hilde ignored them and went on. "I want someone who believes in the good of humanity and seeks to change the world to be a better place. A man with intelligence. Good looking. And a heart-melting smile."

Erika and Gertrud burst out laughing. "You forgot broad shoulders and big biceps. Hilde, you need to get a grip on reality. The man you're looking for doesn't exist."

"What are you saying?" Hilde asked, looking between her two friends.

"There you go again, being naïve and idealistic." Erika smiled at her and then confided, "I would totally conform with a handsome man. Like your step-father, if he were twenty years younger. I'm so excited to see him on stage."

The girls found their seats and Hilde's smile faded as she listened to Gertrud echo Erika's fascination with her step-father, Robert.

"He has such a fabulous voice, and he's quite the charmer. Your mother is lucky to be married to such a handsome and glamorous man. His voice is to die for. Have you thanked him for the tickets?"

"Of course I did," Hilde said. "He told me it was a pleasure for him, but unfortunately, he won't be able to meet us after the performance, because he and Mother have to rush off to the premiere party."

Her friends pouted, and the disappointment on their faces was obvious. Erika was the first one to talk again. "You're such a lucky girl. Your step-father is a famous opera singer and your mother is one of the coolest mom's around. She lets you do anything you want."

Yeah, she's cool all right. So cool that she abandoned her baby girl to marry an opera singer. Hilde had never told either of her friends about her mother abandoning her when she was two years old. How she'd never felt her mother loved her. Or how she was jealous of Robert, because her mother obviously cared more for him than she did for her own daughter.

"The performance is about to start," she said instead.

Their conversation came to an end as the lights in the theater dimmed. Hilde kept her eyes trained on the stage, but her mind was caught up in memories.

She'd been two years old, and her father had been fighting at the frontlines of the Great War when her mother had met the famous opera singer and started an affair with him. Apparently the task of raising a two-year old child was too much of a burden for her mother, because soon after moving in with Robert, she'd dropped Hilde off at her grandmother's house.

Hilde had loved her grandmother dearly, but even living with a woman who'd showered her with love and acceptance hadn't been able to dull the pain her mother had caused by abandoning her.

It wasn't something a little girl could easily forget, and Hilde had made herself a solemn promise to never treat her own little ones so callously. She would never abandon them.

I will always be there for my own children. They won't have to grow up with their grandmother. And they'll never doubt, not for an instant, my love for them.

That thought almost had her bursting out laughing. Just the thought of Marianne – or Annie, the name her mother preferred to be called nowadays – raising grandkids was ludicrous. And Emma? Her step-mom? They didn't even talk to one another. Not since she had left her father's house after a row and moved in with her mother in Berlin two years ago. She'd burned her bridges and any hope of ever returning home to her father and his family.

She sighed, wishing she could do things over. Not leave in a fight. Experience the feeling of being loved again.

Thankfully, Erika grabbed her arm when young Figaro appeared on stage and brought Hilde's mind back to more pleasurable things.

Chapter 8

Q took the tram into Berlin where he had rented a room in a friend's apartment a few months ago. He was a frequent visitor to Berlin on the weekends and found staying there much easier than making the hour-long journey back to his place in Oranienburg after attending a cultural event or going out at night.

He'd known Jakob Goldmann since his days at university, when he had been a tutor for one of Jakob's chemical engineering classes. Despite the age difference of six years, they had become fast friends.

After his PhD, Q had started working for Auer-Gesellschaft and moved to Oranienburg while Jakob was offered a job as a chemical engineer in a big company inside Berlin that produced synthetic materials. His friend was a bright young man and after just a few months on the job, he'd been moved up the ranks and now supervised a team of four workers.

He pondered whether to use his key, but given it was a weekday and he usually only showed up on weekends, he knocked on the door instead. It was early evening and he smiled when Jakob opened the door. "Q! What are you doing here in the middle of the week?"

"Well, since I'm without a job, I decided to come talk to you about our idea," he said while shaking his friend's hand.

Jakob stepped back, ushering Q inside. "What do

you mean you're without a job?"

Q briefly filled his friend in and asked, "Are you still serious about starting up a chemical laboratory? About being self-employed?"

Jakob didn't even hesitate. "I sure am. Are you thinking we should finally stop talking and start doing?"

Q grinned. "Can't think of a better time. I have a lot of free time on my hands right now."

"Coming here on a weekday sure sounds like you have nothing else to do."

"Come on." Q boxed his friend's shoulder. "You want it as much as I do."

They both laughed. They'd been talking about their big plans for years, but due to the bad economic situation in Germany, it had never seemed the right time. Now might be perfect.

"How would we get started?" Jakob asked, gesturing for Q to have a seat on the couch.

Q popped down and said, "Well, we'd need a laboratory space. And equipment."

"There are some vacant buildings just past where I work. We could check there."

"That sounds like a good idea. We'll need two office rooms and a big lab. Or better two. To separate different lines of experiments."

"Yes. And I already know a few people who might give us work." Jakob hopped up and down. They continued talking themselves into a state of excitement and Q could see the laboratory come to life in his mind.

State of the art equipment, newest technology, enough space to do whatever was required to find new solutions to old problems.

After a while, he disappeared into his room and came back with pen and paper to jot down their ideas.

"We can't afford that," Jakob murmured with sagging shoulders as he summed up the numbers Q had written down.

Staring at the staggering number at the bottom of the paper, Q swallowed hard and admitted, "Even if we use all of our combined savings, we don't have enough to get started."

Neither man was rich, but they had both lived well below their means while earning an excellent income from their jobs. Even without the benefit of a paycheck, Q's royalties for having sold the commercial rights to several of his patents in the field of chemistry were more than enough to support him.

"Why don't I visit my bank tomorrow morning and ask for a startup loan?"

Jakob nodded. "It's worth a try."

***

"Doctor Quedlin, I'm sorry, but we're unable to give you a loan at this time," the bank employee said.

"What? Why? I have more than enough collateral to secure the loan..."

"It has nothing to do with that, I'm afraid."

Q raised an eyebrow. "I don't follow. Would you

please explain why you are refusing my request?"

The bank employee looked uncomfortable and squirmed in his seat. "Doctor Quedlin, you are a valued client of our bank, but as you said yourself, you have recently quit your employment and are now depending solely on your royalty checks."

"Which are more than enough to sustain me for the time being." Q pointed to the business plan he'd drafted together with Jakob last night. "Then, with the income the laboratory will generate after an initial startup phase of three months–"

"Doctor Quedlin, a new enterprise is risky and given the current economic situation in Germany, it's not guaranteed you'll be able to meet the credit payments."

Q rolled his eyes. This wasn't going the way he wanted it. "*Mein Herr*, the items we've already discussed as collateral more than meet the value of the money I'm seeking to borrow."

"And several years ago, I would have been happy to finish the paperwork, but the policies of our bank have changed. We now need almost double the security for these types of loans."

"I'll visit another bank."

"You're free to do so, but they will give you the same answer. Due to the declining economy, no bank in Germany is in a position to take huge risks right now."

Huge risks? He was asking for a modest loan of less than one year of Jakob's and his combined income. But this bullheaded bank employee just didn't understand. Taking a deep breath, he said, "If you need more securities, my business partner, Jakob Goldmann, should have more than enough."

The bank employee thinned his lips. "I don't believe that would be a wise call on your part at all."

"And why is that?" Q folded his hands on his lap in an attempt to keep his calm.

"We prefer to do business with Germans."

"Jakob is German."

"Well, he may have acquired a German passport, but he is of Jewish descent."

"You cannot be serious." He all but jumped out of his seat and had the greatest urge to drag the arrogant man across the desk by his tie.

"I am very serious. In fact, I must warn you that continued association with those persons could lead to the seizure of your own accounts."

"You would discriminate against a good citizen because of his race? That is a stupid policy. Awful in fact. All humans were created…"

Q stopped himself before he started a monologue about how ridiculous anti-Semitism was and how he truly believed that communism was a superior ideology. All people deserved to be valued the same and have the same rights, regardless of their race, ancestry, or even gender. No exceptions. But Q realized that those ideas weren't very popular with the bank employee – or the police, he reminded himself – and kept his mouth shut.

"Doctor Quedlin, are you affiliated with the Communist Party?"

Q shook his head. "No. I'm not affiliated with

anyone."

"Then I would strongly advise you to be careful about your statements. If Hitler becomes chancellor, as everyone here hopes, he will make Germany a better and stronger country. He has some very progressive ideas."

"If one wants to believe that, then that is their prerogative."

The bank employee gave him a hard look. "Might I remind you that I have the ability to freeze your account if you insist on supporting the wrong side of the law."

Q closed his eyes for a moment, seeking patience and calm. It was better to keep silent for the moment. He thanked the bank employee and returned to Jakob's apartment.

"How did it go?" his friend asked the moment he walked in the door that evening.

"Not good. I don't have enough security for the loan, and when I mentioned you, I was basically threatened with having my accounts seized."

Jakob turned his face away, but Q knew his friend well enough to feel his pain when he answered, "Well, maybe we should wait until the economy bounces back."

"Maybe." Q sank down onto the couch, a frown marring his brow. "There's more to it than our plans to become self-employed."

"What else has you worried, my friend?"

"You."

"Me?" Jakob finally turned around, and Q didn't like what he read in his friend's eyes. Fear. Shame. Denial.

"Yes. The bank employee's attitude reminded me of how much anti-Semitism is growing in this country. I'm afraid it's going to get much worse."

"I think you're overdramatizing the situation. People are rational beings. *Homo economicus.* They will never follow Hitler's outrageous ideas. This is just a temporary situation."

"You and I we both know the homo economicus is a myth, an idea that works in theory, but not in real life. People flock to Hitler's ideas of renewed grandeur, and they will use anyone and anything as scapegoats if it helps them escape their own misery." Q jumped up and paced the room, running his hand through his short blond curls.

Suddenly, he stopped and planted himself an arm-length distance from Jakob. "Leave the country!" He nearly shouted the words.

His friend stared wide-eyed at him. "Leave my home?"

"Yes. Leave now. You're twenty-three and have your entire life before you. You're young, bright, and graduated in chemistry. You speak fluent Polish, English, and German. You should have no trouble finding a job anywhere in Europe or abroad."

"Now, you're overreacting, Q. I don't want to leave Berlin. My parents love it here. And with my mother's heart condition, I don't think she can handle another dislocation." The entire Goldmann family had emigrated to Germany from Poland sixteen years ago during the Great War.

"Your parents don't have to go."

Jakob's mouth fell open. "I don't want to leave them alone. Things will get better. You'll see."

Q shook his head. "Perhaps. If the economy gets better soon and this great depression doesn't worsen, it might get better."

"I hope it happens sooner than later," Jakob replied.

Q admired the hope his friend espoused, but his gut feeling told him otherwise. A better economy wouldn't be enough. Nor would it come soon enough. Not by a long shot.

Chapter 9

After realizing that his own laboratory wasn't a possibility right then, Q spent many hours thinking about how to best make his stand for peace and a livable future.

He'd been fond of Russia since the October Revolution in 1917. More than once, he'd admired the benefits the Russian people gained once Lenin and the Bolsheviks took over from the autocratic Tsarist regime. But since then little progress had happened. Russia was still mostly rural and needed help to industrialize the country in an effort to make it a power for peace in the future.

Giving all his technical knowledge to the Russian people would be a first step in empowering them to become an industrialized nation. But he had to be careful. During the last years, Germany had become a place where fear and suspicion reigned. Everyone kept to themselves these days, and conversations about the future or viewpoints opposing the mainstream were held exclusively behind closed doors, rather than on the street corners. And in very select company.

One day, he met with a few former fellow students he knew to be fond of the ideas of communism. They were congregating under the guise of a literature club, and everyone had to bring a book to each meeting. Today's topic was the literature of Leopold Tolstoy.

After everyone had arrived, the doors to the

classroom were shut, and they soon started a heated discussion about current politics and the threat the Nazi's posed on life as they knew it.

"But how can we help Mother Russia?"

Q raised his voice. "The best place to start would be in helping Russia defend herself. It's essential to industrialize and militarize Russia in an effort to protect the country from the evil invasions of neighboring countries."

"That is true. With Russia's vast natural resources and land, many other countries are jealous and would love nothing more than to take some of it for themselves."

"Like Japan," said Kurt, a guy with bushy black brows.

"And Hungary or Poland," added Reinhard, a man old enough to be Q's grandfather.

Wilfried held out a hand. "Don't forget Turkey and Austria."

"And Germany," Q said, and everyone stared at him. "Come on, guys. Our country is not beyond taking land during a war. Haven't we started war after war for land and resources?"

"You're right," Kurt agreed. "In the past, everyone who wanted land took it by force. And whoever owned land had to protect it with the blood of its people to keep it. But communism will change this. Humans will realize that they can live in peace, and everyone can still own enough to eat one's fill and be happy."

Everyone nodded, and a slender blonde girl named Johanna stood up, "Yes. The Russian people are good people. They have shown us how to get rid of a regime of injustice. They carry the right *Weltanschauung*. They just don't have the technicians and engineers to carry it out. Now it's our turn to help them."

All of the scientists in the classroom were ready to help and transfer the knowledge and information Russia needed to modernize and keep up with their potential enemies. If tensions in the region increased, it was vital that Russia withstand an invasion from any country that looked upon them as easy prey.

Q liked the idea, but a little warning voice in his head made him raise his concern. "That is all fine and well. But how do we make sure this knowledge is never used against peaceful countries or their own people?"

Everyone started talking at once. When the noise ebbed away, Johanna spoke up again. "They won't. In communism, the people are the government. And they wouldn't do anything to harm themselves."

That sounded like a very rational response. If the true power of a nation was in the hands of its very people, they would look out for the best for everyone. Everyone agreed the first stage of enabling the Russian people to develop was to help them defend themselves.

"Maybe we should emigrate to Russia and oversee the implementation of our work," Michael suggested.

Q shook his head. "No, that's not the best idea. We are more useful if we remain here in Germany to facilitate and promote a lifestyle of peace in both countries. Part of Russia's problem is that it has been cut off from the rest of the world. They need a voice on the outside."

Everyone present agreed, but one question still remained to be answered. "How do we get in touch with the Soviets?"

It was quiet for a moment before Michael said, "There's a Soviet trade mission in Berlin."

"A trade mission?"

"Yes. The official mission is to promote the trade between Germany and Russia." Michael lowered his voice before he continued, "But, the Russian government uses this mission as a way to recruit spies and sell military goods to Germany."

"That is strictly forbidden by the Versailles Treaty," Kurt chimed in.

"Yes. But Germany and Russia signed the Rapallo Treaty in 1922. Two diplomatically isolated and outlawed countries joining forces to help each other."

"That is just a ruse to allow both countries to gain military strength," Johanna cautioned.

"We need more information on the subject," Q suggested.

"I agree," Michael said. "I suggest we ask a volunteer to try and gain access to the trade mission and their secret purpose of existence."

Q immediately raised his hand. "I'll do it."

"Are you sure?" Wilfried asked.

"I am. If Germany is buying weapons from Russia, we need to know about it."

The meeting adjourned a few minutes later, and everyone left the classroom in a hurry. He picked up his copy of *Anna Karenina* and followed the others out of the university building.

He decided to sleep in Berlin instead of returning to Oranienburg. Tomorrow morning, he'd embark on the adventure to reach the secret inner circles of the Soviet trade mission in Berlin.

***

Early the next morning, Q left his apartment. After what happened at Auer-Gesellschaft, he decided some precautions couldn't hurt. He searched the apartment for a disguise and stuffed it into a bag before leaving. Taking a detour to the Berlin Zoo train station, he entered the public restrooms to change his clothing. A stale smell of pee reached his nostrils, and he quickly scanned the toilets for one that was acceptably clean.

He locked the door behind himself and changed into his disguise, black heavy-duty pants and an oversized jacket he'd borrowed from Jakob. His friend might be younger than he was, but his shoulders were much broader. He was also about two inches taller. The dark brown jacket hung on Q's shoulders, making him look like a craftsman who didn't care much about his looks and not like the scientist he was.

Before emerging as, hopefully, an unrecognizable man, he pulled his hat low over his brow, covering his signature curls.

Half an hour and several detours later, he entered the Soviet trade mission at Unter den Linden and asked to speak with the commercial attaché. He pretended to be the owner of a craftsman's workshop seeking opportunities to trade goods with Russia.

The receptionist noted his name and request before she instructed him to seat himself in the waiting area. Almost an hour went by before a man in his fifties approached him. "Herr Quedlin?"

Q stood up and surveyed the man in front of him. "Yes. I am Wilhelm Quedlin. Herr Handelsattaché?"

The man didn't answer but gestured for Q to follow him. They took seats in an office, and the other man asked, "How may I help you?"

"I was hoping to speak to whomever is in charge of scientific operations and exchange of knowledge."

The commercial attaché raised his brows. "What does the owner of a craftsman's workshop know about science?"

"Sir, I'm actually not a craftsman."

"I thought so. Your outfit is actually pretty ridiculous."

Q sucked in a breath. He'd hoped to be convincing in his role play. "I didn't want to be seen coming here."

Now the other man seemed to be interested and leaned back in his seat. He lit a cigar and puffed out a few smoke circles while he scrutinized Q. After a while, he finally said, "So what do you really want?"

"I'm a chemical engineer and would like to offer my knowledge and my inventions to the Russian people."

The commercial attaché narrowed his eyes and shook his head. "That could be a trick. Who tells me you're sincere?"

Q thought quickly and answered, "I worked with several Russian scientists while at university. One of them was Dmitry Zelinsky. He's now a professor at the Moscow State University. He will vouch for me." *I hope he remembers me.*

The man stared into Q's eyes, apparently debating whether he should believe him or not. Then he spoke up, "Come back next month. In the meantime, we will verify your credentials."

"That's fair." He handed the man a copy of the article he'd written about the gas masks. "Here's a small offering for you to see that I'm serious."

The man took the paper and bid him leave. "Thank you."

Chapter 10

Hilde finished the file in front of her and stacked it on top of the others she'd processed that morning on the corner of her desk. She stretched her arms above her head and glanced at the large clock at the head of the room. Almost lunch time.

She cleared away the pens on her desk and reached for the sack lunch she normally brought along before heading for the small breakroom, waving at Erika and Gertrud to join her. Her company was too small to have a canteen and eating out was expensive.

Gertrud sat down next to her, disgruntled. "They're threatening to fire some employees at the end of the month."

"I know. I heard. In this bad economy, the company is having a hard time staying afloat. People prefer to save the insurance fee and count on their luck," Hilde answered, opening her lunch box.

"The entire country is sinking. The unemployment rate is now nearing forty percent. Forty percent! Can you even believe such a thing has been allowed to happen?" Erika asked, shaking her head in disgust.

Every evening on her way home from work, Hilde passed the lines of people standing outside the soup kitchens and the job centers. The lines were growing, and the people standing in them were looking more desperate each day that passed. Hilde always felt a pang of empathy for them and thanked God every day that she still held a job. Not a great one, but one that allowed her to contribute her share to the household expenses. While she would love to move out on her own, it wouldn't happen anytime soon. It was just too expensive.

"Something needs to be done, or we'll soon be a nation of beggars," a woman from the sales force said in a loud voice. She'd joined their table together with two older men Hilde had seen several times, but didn't remember their names.

"The Allied Powers are to blame for this," one of the men said, and suddenly, everyone in the room looked at their table, and you could hear a needle drop.

"Yes, yes," several people said in agreement.

The man spoke up again. "What gives them the right to choke the very life from the German people? Their reparations are outright dehumanizing."

The head of the sales force had entered the room, and his big bulging face turned a deep shade of purple when he heard his subordinates talking like this.

Hilde feared for a moment they'd have to face his disapproval, but he chimed right into the conversation. "The Versailles Treaty is crippling our country. I was a young lad during the last war, and yet I'll have to work my entire life to pay back a debt I didn't incur."

"I agree. Why don't the French, British, and Russians try to exist under such harsh conditions and see what happens?"

"We need a strong leader to stand up for Germany and stop this madness."

Hilde instinctively ducked her head and stayed out

of the conversation. This wouldn't go anywhere reasonable.

"Only a strong chancellor can bring our nation back to her former strength and glory. The war is long over. It's about time for someone to step in and send the Entente Alliance back to where they came from."

"With their tails between their legs," Erika added, and the others applauded.

"One of our customers told me the Allied Powers want more money. What was agreed is not enough for them and they're mounting an attack against Germany to extract even more. They want us reduced to nothing more than slaves." The head of the sales force said.

Another man chimed in. "We need to stop this now before it cannot be undone."

Hilde ate her lunch, questioning how much of this talk was actually based on facts and how much was pure street talk. She vaguely remembered having read somewhere that payment of reparations had been stopped the year before.

"Hitler is our man." This came from a gentleman at the end of the table. "He's not a puppy of the Allied Forces, and he's promising employment for everyone. His first step is to build Autobahns all over Germany, to increase mobility of people and goods."

"Can you imagine how it would be to drive a car from Berlin all the way to Stuttgart on a road that actually deserves that name? Without potholes, curves or intersections?" One of the men said with shining eyes and the conversation turned towards cars and the promise of affordable cars for everyone.

The girls shook their heads, quickly finished their lunch, and left the breakroom. As soon as they were out of earshot, Erika lowered her voice to a whisper, "I heard that the British want to take over Germany because their island is slowly sinking into the North Sea."

Hilde gasped.

"And did you know the French soldiers eat little kids? We sure don't want them in our country," Gertrud added with a shudder.

Those statements of her friends were so bizarre and far-fetched she figured they must be joking, but both of them showed only seriousness on their faces. What if they told the truth? Could it be?

Erika and Gertrud seemed well informed and invested in their opinions, whereas Hilde herself had no opinion whatsoever. Her father, a very politically oriented individual, had always taught her politics was no place for a woman.

But he's miles away and being ignorant isn't getting you anywhere. Maybe you need to become better informed.

"See you girls after work," Erika said, drawing her from her mental meanderings.

"See you. Have a lovely afternoon," Gertrud said and headed back to her desk.

Hilde was left alone, her mind spinning with everything she'd just heard. What was truth and what was just a fantastic story devised to play upon the fears of the people?

In this instance, she decided to learn about politics. After work, she stopped at the newspaper vendor stationed on the corner and purchased the *Berliner Morgenpost* and a big notebook. As soon as she arrived home, she read the paper from cover to cover, paying special attention to everything about current politics.

Organized as she was, she began a meticulous study of the different political parties, making a chart with the programs and beliefs each one stood for and cutting out pictures of key people to put on her new "learning wall." The more she read about politics, the more interested she became and the more she wanted to know.

Her notebook became her canvas, and like an artist, she began to paint a picture with words of the political environment in Germany over the next weeks. Beneath the picture of Hindenburg, she wrote the words *Weimarer Republic*. He represented the current and ineffective government of Germany. Summarizing his achievements was easy. *Failure* was all she needed. The current government was failing in every aspect she could see. A change was needed. But who could offer a change for the better?

Three main players competed for votes: Adolf Hitler, head of the NSDAP - Nazi Party; Otto Wels, head of the SPD -Socialist Democrat Party; and Ernst Thälmann, leader of the KPD - Communist Party.

To the picture of each of the three men, she added a small statement that summed up each party's core beliefs. This took some effort, and she honed the statement several times over the next days and weeks, whenever she collected new information.

Beneath the picture of Hitler, she wrote the words: *Führerprinzip* - Strong Leadership. Nationalistic,

Economy directed by industry. Strong military. Superiority of the Aryan race.

Under the picture of Wels, she added the words: Reform. Opponent of Anti-Semitism. Egalitarian for economy and industry.

That left only the Communist party picture of Thälmann, under which she wrote: Dictatorship of the proletariat. Equality of men and women, but against the Republic and Democracy.

Hilde sighed. Germany was going under, and as far as she was concerned, none of the popular parties would be her salvation. It was much more possible either the left or the right would lead her into complete destruction.

Still, she eyed her work in progress and felt a small sense of accomplishment. At least she now understood the political climate around her and was determined to keep abreast of what was happening and hopefully make an educated decision if the time came to do so.

Chapter 11

Q stared at his desk covered in papers with scribbled formulas and sketches of devices not yet in existence. *Somewhere must be the missing link! I just haven't found it yet.* Not able to focus anymore, he decided to take a break and go for a short walk to freshen up his mind.

While he was still angry with Director Hoffmann for treating him unjustly and firing him without reason, he couldn't deny that he felt better than he had in years. The burden of holding down a demanding job and having to subordinate his research to commercial interests had fallen like a stone from his shoulder.

Finally, he had all the time in the world to follow his passion and work exclusively on his own research, making inventions in the field of electronics, chemistry, and radio-transmission. And while he was thankful for that, the memory of the arbitrary treatment was a constant thorn in his side. A thorn that spurred him on to work harder and devote his time to inventing as many useful things as possible to help foster peace in Europe while also helping his Russian friends to make the Soviet Union a power that could oppose Germany in the upcoming war.

War hadn't been announced, and everybody around him seemed to believe the Great War had been the last one, but Q feared his country was headed for another war sooner or later. And the wise thing to do was to prepare for that day. One could never be too prepared.

That knowledge fueled his determination, and he decided not to look for another job. As his royalties were still coming in regularly, with more hopefully being added, he was in the comfortable position of not having to work for his living. Instead, he used all his time and energy for research and made some major advancement into the usage of the oxides of nitrogen.

It was already dark on this winter afternoon, and he shuffled his feet in the freshly fallen snow as he considered his options. Recently, he'd diversified his research work and experimented with the possibility of using radio to operate devices or machines by remote control. Another of his ideas was to use sound waves and radio transmissions to detect obstacles. But something was missing.

Then he heard it.

"Who-o-o, who-o-o."

Q squinted his eyes in an effort to see the owl, but it was too dark, and the bird probably was sitting in a tree blocked from his view. As a kid, when he'd lived with his parents in the countryside near Magdeburg, he'd seen many owls and bats.

Bats! That's it!

He turned around and hurried home.

A few years back, an American physicist had proven that bats used ultrasound to orient themselves. As he hurried, his scientist mind envisioned a means to locate things like air planes, ships and even vehicles using a system of echoes similar to the one bats used, but viable for long range detection. Radio waves.

He was itching to go over his formulas and set up

some experiments, but as soon as he entered the building, his landlady appeared out of nowhere. *I bet she has some kind of tenant detection system.*

"Doctor Quedlin, do you have one moment?"

No, he didn't. "Sure, ma'am."

She entered her flat and returned with a large envelope in hand. "This came with the daily post."

"Thank you, ma'am." He reached for the envelope containing an official looking seal and wanted to sprint up the stairs to his own apartment. But he hadn't taken into account the supreme curiosity of his landlady, who held onto the envelope, asking, "What is it?"

Q had no interest in divulging the contents to his landlady, so he answered nonchalantly, "Technical papers I need for my work."

"Oh," she said, her curiosity obviously not yet satisfied. "Did you notice we had another power outage today? This is happening a lot lately. Would you have any idea why?"

He tried his best to look worried and dispel her suspicion. "Yes, ma'am, I noticed. It's quite a nuisance. The power company must be having a problem somewhere along the line. Hopefully, they will get it fixed sooner than later. Good evening, ma'am."

With a nod, he snapped the envelope and turned on his heel before his grin could give him away. Then he rushed up the stairs, taking three steps at a time.

If his landlady had the faintest idea the frequent outages were a direct result of his electrical experiments, he'd be out on the street in no time at all. She was suspicious enough since he'd lost his job, and he was sure she would be anything but happy if she ever found out he used his apartment to conduct scientific research that sometimes involved explosive substances or caused minor blips like electrical outages.

Inside his flat, he tore the envelope open. It was from the patent office, and he laughed as he looked over the paper inside.

***

Q gathered up his most recent studies and stuffed them into his briefcase. Glancing at his watch, he smiled. In half an hour he would meet his friends Jakob, Otto, and Leopold. With his recent acquisition of a Ford Köln automobile, the journey from Oranienburg to Berlin took less than twenty minutes.

Just in time, he parked his automobile at the curb next to the bar where his friends already waited for him. They'd known each other since university and had since met in irregular intervals to discuss the newest developments in science. Jokingly, they'd given themselves the name *Tüftlerclub* as the four of them liked to invent, research, and tinker.

After proudly presenting his new car and enjoying the admiration of his friends, they stepped inside and ordered Schnitzel with potato salad. When everyone had a beer in hand, Otto addressed the one topic that everyone in Germany seemed to talk about today: Hitler's *Machtergreifung* – seizure of power.

"Did you see the headlines?" Otto asked excitedly.

"Everyone has," Leopold answered. "Hitler has seized control of the government."

Since the radio broke the news last night that Hitler had proclaimed himself the new chancellor of Germany along with his NSDAP party acquiring several high-ranking cabinet posts, an unusual excitement had captured every person in Germany. Q had perceived that people seemed to be one of two persuasions: happily excited or very upset with the Nazi party.

"Can you believe that within a few hours, Swastika flags have appeared on basically every building?" Q asked.

"Now everything will change for the better," Otto said. "Hitler will get us out of the unjust Versailles Treaty and make us a proud and powerful nation once again."

Leopold nodded eagerly. "You're right. The reparations imposed upon Germany after the Great War were nothing more than a way to humiliate our nation. It's time to stop that."

"Come on, guys. The reparations were ended last year during the Lausanne conference. You can't blame them for the bad economy." Jakob tried to bring the discussion back to the facts, but neither Leopold nor Otto wanted to hear them right now.

"They sure didn't help. I hope Hitler can do everything he's promised."

"Everything?" Q asked, looking around the table. "What about his racism and anti-Semitism?"

Leopold and Otto looked at Jakob and sobered a bit. "Neither of us agree on that part of his ideas, but it's nothing to be afraid of. Things are never as bad as they look. Besides, I think that type of stuff was just talk."

Q's gut twisted, and he shrugged, "I sure hope so. But only time will tell."

His friends had always been more carefree than he was, and they'd teased him time after time for overthinking. Even Jakob seemed fairly nonchalant about the situation, although there was a new tension about him that Q hadn't noticed months earlier.

Deep down, Q knew Hitler was a fanatic, willing to go to extremes to make his beliefs come true. Much like Q himself, who would sacrifice almost anything for his science. But while Q always intended to serve humankind, he doubted that Hitler acted on the same maxim.

Their conversation switched from politics to science and after the second beer, they started reciting funny rhymes and spoonerisms.

"Es klapperten die Klapperschlangen

bis ihre Klappern schlapper klangen."

Q stood up, "I have another one." Then he recited:

"She sells sea shells;

It's sea shells she sells."

When Q drove home, he had thoroughly enjoyed the evening with his friends, but for some reason, he couldn't get rid of the feeling that the events yesterday had irreparably changed the course of history. But even he couldn't imagine that this day would, decades later, be named the most fateful day of the century.

***

The next week, Q visited the Soviet trade mission again. This time, the commercial attaché was happy to see him and introduced himself with the name Herr Iwanov.

"Doctor Quedlin, what a pleasure to see you. Please take a seat."

Two more men were already sitting at the small table in the middle of the room and gave him a friendly nod.

After some small talk, Herr Iwanov said, "We have made contact with Mr. Zelinksy, and he confirmed to us that you are a loyal believer in the ideals of the October Revolution and Communism. Our scientists also double-checked the information you provided in regards to the gas mask. It is of high quality and very useful to the Russian people. Therefore, we would like to suggest an 'official' cooperation, if that is what you were after."

Q nodded. "Thank you, Herr Iwanov. That is indeed high praise."

"We are unable to offer you much money, but..."

Q shook his head. "You misunderstand my reason for being here. I don't want money."

Everyone in the room looked at him, and it was so quiet you could hear a needle drop. "You don't?"

"No, I am doing this for the greater good." He missed the looks the Soviet men shared with one another. "I want to help humanity, and hopefully, prevent another devastating war."

"You feel war is a possibility?" one of the men inquired.

Q nodded. "Yes. I believe the new government in Germany is headed directly there. Every day, Hitler is keeping a tighter rein on things and getting rid of unwanted opposition. I'm very sure he will do everything in his power to make his dreams come true."

The other man scrutinized Q for a moment. "If you believe Hitler is here to stay and is as dangerous as you say, you must be aware that working with us will make you a traitor and put you in grave danger."

A shiver ran down Q's spine. He hadn't given that aspect much thought when he'd decided to gather intelligence for the Russians, but after the *Machtergreifung* last week, he'd had to re-think his decision. Even though it wasn't technically illegal to give his own work to other nations, the current powers wouldn't forgive anyone working against them.

He squared his shoulders before he answered, "I have given this possibility some thought, and have come to the conclusion that the greater good is more important than my own well-being."

The three men nodded with admiration, and Herr Iwanov said, "That is a very rare and courageous attitude you're showing. But why bring your information and skills to us? Why Russia and not another country? After all, our countries were enemies in the last war?"

A grin spread over Q's face. "I believe Germany has been enemies with every other country around. But to answer your question, I've thoroughly studied the other European nations, and I believe Russia is the only country that will use my inventions and expertise with the good of the people in mind. I wish for my discoveries to be used to help my fellow man in a peaceful manner."

The men exchanged incredulous glances. "Your answer shows that you're a scientist and not a politician. Given the chance, men will always act against one another."

Q looked around the room and asked, "Will they? Hasn't the Bolshevism abolished the selfish egoism of a few and replaced it with a government of the people?" He shook his head, answering his own rhetorical question. "I merely want the best for myself and others, and there are many more men and women who think the same way."

Chapter 12

During one of Q's meetings with his Russian contact, whom he only knew by the name Pavel, the agent asked him, "Would you be willing to travel to Paris on a mission?"

"Paris?" Q raised an eyebrow. "That's in France."

"Yes, it is, Q. As you suggested yourself, the Nazi government is problematic, to say the least. They are an unknown force in the equilibrium of powers and seem to care little for maintaining peace in the region."

"And what does that have to do with Paris," Q asked.

"Our government has taken up negotiations with the French – absolutely confidentially and unofficially, of course. We are seeking to exchange knowledge to better prepare all neighboring European countries for war against Germany."

Q nodded. "That makes sense, but what role do I play in there?"

Pavel leaned across the table in the crowded café and lowered his voice. "We have received a request for help from a group of French chemical engineers who are working closely with gas warfare. With your experience and expertise, we believe you can help them solve the problem."

A flattered smile curled Q's lips, and a tingle of excitement rushed through his veins. This would be his first important mission and to France no less. He'd learned French at school but was in no way fluent in the language.

"I would be honored to help."

The Russian agent explained the details of the trip, and when he had finished, Q asked, "How should I explain my trip? I can't tell the authorities I'm going to help some French scientists to find ways to detect and counteract gas warfare. Can I?"

The thought of what might happen if he was caught and the authorities learned his true reason for going to Paris froze his blood.

Pavel grinned and then asked, "Do you know how to ski?"

"Ski? Yes. Why?"

"To hide the true reason for your trip."

Q was so nervous he had difficulties following the words of his counterpart. *Skiing in Paris? Don't they have a better plan?*

"We have arranged for a hotel in Klosters. You'll take a weeklong skiing holiday. Switzerland has always remained neutral in every conflict and nobody will suspect any political motives if you travel there. Go skiing, have fun, and then continue your trip to Paris without telling anyone. You'll find all the details in here."

The agent handed him an envelope. "Apart from travel documents and instructions, there are enough Swiss Francs and French Francs in there to cover your travel expenses for this trip."

Q eyed the envelope suspiciously. Being paid for his trip didn't mesh with his idealistic motifs of working for the greater good. "I don't want to be paid for my help."

The agent pushed the envelope into Q's hands. "Take it. Use the money with our thanks."

Q argued with the man a few more minutes and then capitulated. "Very well, but I'll only use the money to travel to Paris to meet with these engineers and will return the rest at our next meeting. I will pay for the skiing holiday myself."

"As you wish." The agent smiled and disappeared, while Q sat in the café trying to fully process what just happened. He didn't dare open the envelope in there and stuffed it into his briefcase before he paid and left.

As soon as Q returned to his apartment in Oranienburg, he tore the envelope open and rushed to read the details of his trip. He was to leave in a few days, and his mind was buzzing with the plans he needed to make. And the excuses he needed to have ready.

Because he'd never heard from the police again about the investigation against him for industrial espionage, he was fairly certain it had been closed, but a small doubt remained. He didn't want to poke the sleeping lion, but not knowing the outcome made him uncomfortable. Thus, he sat down to write a letter to the police asking about the official outcome of his investigation.

He cringed as he imagined how different an interrogation by the SA Brownshirts or the SS Schutzstaffel might look like from what he had experienced with the police were they to discover his true reason for travelling to Paris. Those paramilitary wings of the Nazi party were known to punch first and ask questions later, and Q was certain he didn't want to be the subject of their attention. In any form.

***

Q tried his best to enjoy his two days of skiing vacation in Klosters but was too nervous. His mission occupied his mind every waking moment. His trip to Paris on the night train went smoothly, and the next morning, he met with the French scientists.

They were all friendly and intelligent men, but unfortunately, their English was a lot worse than he'd hoped for causing several minor hiccups in the course of the next days. But what drove him nearly insane were the work habits of his French colleagues. Every little detail required an hour long discussion before it could be implemented.

If they start another fruitless discussion, I'll start screaming. Have those Frenchmen never heard of efficiency?

At home, people got right to the heart of the problem and fixing it. Name the problem. Think of a solution. Test it. If it didn't work, repeat. There was no need to discuss all the possible solutions when one could just go and test them out. But the French worked the opposite way.

When presented with a new problem, they talked about it. A lot. Usually, about ten minutes into the discussion, his colleagues forgot about his presence and switched to their mother language. Back at home, he'd thought his understanding of the French language was passable, but now he knew better.

As soon as his colleagues inevitably started talking at the same time and sped up their speaking, he lost track of the conversation, and his understanding was reduced to mumble jumble.

He leaned back and observed the three chemical engineers and found himself staring in amazement at their heated discussion. It seemed perfectly normal for them to raise their voices at each other, shouting for hours without apparent reason about a problem, just to later congratulate each other for coming up with a solution. It was peculiar, but it apparently worked.

Their methods were so much less efficient than those he was used to, but to his utter surprise, they managed to come up with solutions anyway. Sometimes amazing solutions he wouldn't have thought of.

The one part of their day Q truly enjoyed was lunch. From the first day, he fell in love with the French cuisine and the wine. Rather than a hurried half an hour or even a respectable hour for lunch, the Frenchmen took a full two hours, sometimes more. Every time they ate, it was a celebration and Q fully participated. It was such an amazing experience to savor the food instead of gulping it down without thinking. His colleagues even urged him to join them in drinking a glass of wine during lunch because it was good for the health.

This was another peculiar French habit. In Germany, you could be fired for drinking at work, but here? They'd probably fire you if you didn't have a glass of wine with your meal. Suspicious at first, Q soon started to like this habit. One small glass of wine – not more – stimulated his brain and loosened his inhibitions enough to give his colleagues a taste of his not-so-perfect French language skills.

"Vous parlez français!" Antoine Dubois said, and Q nodded proudly. From that moment on, the ice was broken and Q was accepted as a friend. "Je suis Antoine," his colleague offered, introducing himself. In response, Q answered, "Mon nom suis Wilhelm, mais m'apelle Q."

Everyone laughed at his faulty usage of French grammar, but it didn't matter. From now on, he was part of their team, and they did their best to make him feel welcome in Paris.

The next day they invited him to dinner after work and as always, they talked about anything and everything under the sun. Soon, the discussion turned to politics and Antoine asked him, "Your new chancellor, Hitler, he is temporary?"

Q thought for a moment and then shook his head. "At this point in time, I'm afraid not. He has a lot of support from the military and the people."

"But his *Machtergreifung*...there was nothing democratic about it. Won't he be called to account?"

"In the old Germany yes, but we have a new Germany now." Q could see the worry on their faces; one he secretly shared.

"Just last week the news said books are being burned, and opponents hunted down. *Gleichschaltung* they call it," another of his colleagues said.

Q nodded. "The word literally means to synchronize

or bring into line. I believe the Nazi party is trying to bring about a specific doctrine and way of thinking. They want more control."

"There have been reports of people being arrested who openly criticized the Nazi form of government."

Q hadn't heard such reports but wasn't surprised. "Many of my fellow compatriots don't take Hitler and what he's trying to do seriously. Most seem to think he is all talk and exaggeration just for show."

"But you don't?" Antoine asked.

"I wouldn't be here if I did." He grinned. "I believe he is very dangerous. He's talked about expelling all thirty political parties out of Germany. He's after absolute power and authority over my country."

"And what happens when he gets it?"

"May God prevent this." Q didn't have an answer for that question, but he feared the man's lust for power would send Germany and the whole of Europe into an inferno.

His colleagues seemed to have filled their need for information about German politics and changed the topic to the latest shows and events in Paris. Their conversation was a mishmash of French and English, and Q had difficulty keeping up. His mind started to wander as someone in the restaurant shouted, "Turn the radio louder. The German Parliament building was destroyed today."

Everyone in the room stopped talking, and Q listened in growing horror at how quickly the political situation in his country was coming unraveled.

Today, Monday, February 27, 1933, the Reichstag building in Berlin, the capital of Germany, was set ablaze in an event that is being deemed arson.

Our reporter in Berlin confirms that a mentally ill Dutchman has been arrested. He was found hiding inside the burning building.

The main chamber of the building was completely engulfed in flames when authorities arrived. No word yet on what was used to start the fire.

Our man in Berlin has forwarded the following statement by Hermann Göring, the second most powerful man in the current Nazi regime, regarding today's events.

"This is the beginning of a Communist upheaval. They will start a revolution now. We cannot miss one minute to strike back!"

German President Paul von Hindenburg, at the urging of Chancellor Hitler, has been asked to issue an emergency decree suspending all civil liberties in order to counter the illegal and horrific actions of the Communist party.

Chancellor Hitler himself spoke to the people shortly after several additional arrests were made. "Now, there will be no mercy. Whoever is against us will be slaughtered. The German nation will not understand if we are kind. Every Communist will be shot, wherever we find him. The Communist members of parliament have to be hanged tonight. Everyone will be arrested who works for the Communists."

We will keep you apprised of the situation, but it appears that Germany is getting ready to declare war on its own citizens. I'm sure I'm not alone in asking how they have *come to a conclusion about who set this fire so quickly. Maybe because this event was orchestrated by the Nazi party to gain support and legitimize their dictatorship and unconstitutional takeover of the government last month.*

This is another setback in the French-German relations, and I'm sure our government will pass a statement soon.

Q's colleagues stared at him, eyes wide open, waiting for his reaction. "Well…it seems our mutual concerns about Hitler and the Nazis have come to pass."

Despite the horrific news, he found it amusing at how differently the news had been presented to the French people. In Germany, the virtues of the government to take fast and decisive actions would have been celebrated, the perpetrators of this crime painted as monsters.

And it seemed that the rest of the world wasn't quite sure if the rhetoric coming out of the Nazi leadership was to be believed. The radio speaker had even insinuated a plot by the Nazis.

"How could Göring and Hitler accuse the Communist party of this act? There was no evidence? What about the Dutchman?" Everyone had questions to ask.

"Because it benefits them to do so," Q replied, still reeling from the impact of what he just learned.

Later in his hotel room, he thought a long time about the implications and what would come next.

The shocks continued the next day when the *Reichstagsbrandverordnung* was passed. Hitler had succeeded in getting the civil liberties and all constitutional rights of the German citizens revoked.

"What does this mean for your countrymen?" Antoine asked the next morning over coffee as the report came in.

"Basically, it means that the SA now has the right to arrest anyone without giving a reason. There will be no legal protection or any chance of defending oneself against false accusations." A shiver ran down his spine as Q remembered when he'd been accused of high treason last fall. Under these new laws, he would have been shot on sight, or worse.

"So, the authorities will arrest everyone they suspect has ties to a political party other than the Nazis?" another colleague asked in horror.

Q nodded. "That's what it sounds like."

"But where will they imprison that many people?"

Q was wondering that himself, but he didn't have an answer.

The next day he was due to leave Paris, but his colleagues didn't want to let him go. They generously offered for him to stay and they'd help him find a job in Paris.

"Although your French is awful," Antoine grinned, "I'm sure any company involved in nitrogen research would gladly employ you if you come recommended by anyone of our group."

"I appreciate your offer, I really do, but my place is in Berlin."

"It's too dangerous for you to return to Germany. I'm sure your stay here would be considered as opposing the government."

Q had weighed the risks most of the night. He was worried that his past accusations might come back to haunt him. Everyone and anyone suspected of supporting the Communist Party would now be open to prosecution.

But in the end, he knew he could be of the most use to his friends in Russia, and for peace, if he returned to Berlin. As much as he wanted to stay safe in Paris, he wanted to do his bit to help overthrow the Nazi regime. And he could not do that from inside France.

"Thank you, my friend, but I must return home." He left in the evening to return to Klosters, once again thankful the Russian agent had arranged to disguise his trip as a skiing vacation. No one would suspect him of engaging in any subversive activity in Switzerland.

When he boarded the train two days later to return to Berlin, he passed the time by reviewing his accomplishments the last few days. He'd been able to help the French scientists with their problem detecting a rare nitrogen gas, and he knew they'd prepare their country to defend itself in the upcoming war. A war that was inevitable at this point. In exchange, he'd learned many things he could use for his current projects.

Q leaned back in the empty train compartment and watched the beautiful countryside passing by. The train was driving north alongside the Rhine river, passing breathtaking scenery. Steamships traveled the brownish river, fast ships going downstream and slowly trudging ships going upstream.

Green, forest covered hills rose to both sides of the

river, and every now and then, they passed a marvelous castle high up on the mountains.

The cradle of German culture. He remembered the legend of the beautiful siren Lorelei sitting on the cliff high above the Rhine and combing her golden hair. With her strikingly beautiful voice, she attracted shipmen and caused them to crash on the rocks.

The lyrics to the legend had become a well-known folk song, and he whistled its melody.

Die schönste Jungfrau sitzet

dort oben wunderbar;

ihr gold'nes Geschmeide blitzet,

sie kämmt ihr goldnes Haar;

sie kämmt es mit goldenem Kamme

und singt ein Lied dabei,

das hat eine wundersame,

gewaltige Melodei.

Den Schiffer im kleinen Schiffe

ergreift es mit wildem Weh;

er schaut nicht die Felsenriffe,

er schaut nur hinauf in die Höh'.

Ich glaube, die Wellen verschlingen

am ende noch Schiffer und Kahn;

und das hat mit ihrem Singen

die Lorelei gethan.

(find the English translation in the Acknowledgements)

He sneered. The NSDAP party was like a siren, distracting everyone with her alluring song and ultimately causing the whole country to crash. After witnessing firsthand how the news reports were being twisted by the German leadership, he feared things were about to get much worse.

Any sense of morality was stripped away by the unconstitutional revoking of the German constitution. The government was no longer lawful, nor did they have any restrictions being placed upon them.

A sense of freedom flooded Q in recognizing that fact. He had always prided himself on being a man of ethics and high morals. But faced with a lawless government intent on stripping all rights and liberties from the people who might oppose them, he no longer felt morally bound to act within their law.

Before this day, he had only given his own intellectual property to his Russian friends, but now...he was actively thinking about engaging in what any intelligent person would deem industrial espionage. And he didn't feel the least bit guilty. The Nazi regime had to be stopped. At any cost.

Chapter 13

Hilde sat at her desk, wondering why all of the employees had been called to attend a meeting. Since January, the threat of firings had augmented every day, driving tensions high and creating an atmosphere of fear.

Every morning, she entered her office with a knotted stomach from the sheer amount of negativity inside the company. People didn't smile and greet anymore. Instead, they ducked their heads and silently walked by.

Nobody stopped longer than necessary at the water cooler or gathered beside the coffee machine for a little chat. No, everyone seemed to be frozen by fear, trying to work as hard as possible to impress their superiors.

Glancing at the clock, her stomach tightened as she saw it was only a few minutes until the meeting was to start. Taking a deep breath, she left her desk to join the other employees as they gathered in the large meeting hall.

No one dared to talk aloud, but the nervous whispers told Hilde everyone was afraid they were about to be fired in one large group. She was quite confident. She processed the insurance claims, and her department was swamped with work. They surely wouldn't fire her. She bit her lip. Surely.

Erika waved her over. She worked in the accounting department and had often mentioned that the company wasn't doing as poorly as the managers made it seem. At least the company managed to still make a small profit every month.

A few minutes later, the director greeted them somberly and started his speech, "As most of you know, times have been hard, and while we have done our best to cut back on expenses, we have now come to the point where we are forced to prune the company of dead wood. We have spent a considerable amount of time looking over our current employees, and I'm proud to say that we will be continuing with the right people in place to be successful in the coming months and years."

Hilde was stunned. The director was speaking about firing people and seemed to be happy about that fact. Her stomach churned as his words replayed in her head, but before she could wonder about whether or not she'd done enough to keep her job, the director continued his speech.

"I know this decision means some extra work for the remaining employees, but I'm sure everyone of you will proudly make this small sacrifice for our nation and our Führer."

Holy hell! What is this man talking about?

"We have decided to free our company of the heavy burden of all employees who don't belong to the superior Aryan race. You are to retrieve your personal effects and pick up your final paycheck at the recruitment office within the hour."

A cacophony of voices arose, but the director had already stepped down from the podium and disappeared. Hilde glanced around at the stunned faces of her co-workers. Some wore smug sneers. Others – the fired ones – wore a look of desperation that clawed at her heart. The majority looked shell shocked. They avoided her eyes and looked down to the floor. Head ducking seemed to be the new ability to master.

Hilde whispered to Gertrud, "Can you believe this? They fired everyone independent of their job title or their tenure with the company. Just because of their race."

Erika didn't seem to mind. She had some exciting news to share. She found Hilde and Gertrud amidst the multitude of people and joined them. "Girls, we have to celebrate! You're looking at the new head of the accounting department."

Gertrud raised a brow. "How's that?"

"Everyone else except me and the two interns have been laid off, so it was only natural I'd get the promotion." She beamed with pride, and her happiness would have been contagious if it weren't for the dire circumstances.

Hilde couldn't hide the disgusted grimace she knew was settled on her face. "What's wrong with you? How can you be happy now?"

Erika merely shrugged. "You have to take the opportunities when they appear. I can't do anything about the company's decision, so I do myself a favor by going along with it. I would never have been promoted so fast if it weren't for this lucky serendipity."

"Lucky?" Hilde hissed, unable to hide the emotion seizing her system. "Don't you even care that the people you've worked with have lost their jobs? And for no other reason than being Jews?"

"Sure, I feel bad, but I'm also being practical here. I have to think about myself. Besides, the company doesn't want them. They should go somewhere else. Someplace where no one will care they're Jews. The Führer says we're better off without them."

Gertrud put a hand on Hilde's shoulder and sent her a better-keep-your-mouth-shut look. She swallowed down her sharp answer and merely scowled at Erika, who was unconcerned by her friend's disapproval and advised, "You should be thankful you weren't fired. Stop whining over the fate of other people. Everyone needs to be looking after themselves these days."

Then she turned and walked away, already practicing the determined walk of a head of accounting. Gertrud grabbed Hilde's elbow and dragged her toward the stairs. "I'm not happy about this any more than you are, but Erika is partly right. Don't talk about your disapproval or make waves. Not one word. You don't want to appear as a *Judenfreund* who sides with the Jews, or you could end up getting hauled away by the SA. Most of us are shocked at what just occurred, but we're also glad we got to keep our jobs. Look around you. Many of these people have families to provide for."

Hilde nodded, following Gertrud as everyone filed back to his or her desk. She listened half-heartedly to the whispers, frustrated and feeling powerless as she heard more than one person mentioning it was the Jews' fault that Germany ached under the grip of the Great Depression.

"The Jews have been stealing our jobs for years now.

We didn't ask for them to come here. We've been too nice, allowing them to take German jobs. It's time for us to rise up and take back our country. They should all go back to where they came from."

Hilde tried to keep her silence, but her colleagues were talking such nonsense, she couldn't resist trying to reason with them. "You're not being fair. The Jews have helped Germany in many ways."

"Really? By taking our jobs?"

"We welcomed them with open arms at one point," she argued.

"Well, now we want them to leave us alone. Instead of destroying our country, they need to go home and fix theirs."

"Most of them don't have a home to go back to. Their families have lived in Germany for many generations or has that completely skipped your minds?" She was growing agitated at the absurdity of what was coming out of her colleagues' mouths.

She entered her department, and her heart broke a little when she passed the glass door to the treasury department and saw Adam Eppstein standing in front of his desk with sagging shoulders. The normally cheerful man was a picture of misery, and hatred for the Nazis rose up inside of her. Adam Eppstein had been the one to train her when she first joined the company. He'd soon been promoted to head of treasury, and Hilde had always valued him as a fellow employee, boss, and human. His only fault was being a Jew.

"*Herr* Eppstein, can I help you collect your things?"

He said nothing, still in shock, staring blankly into the air. When he didn't answer or move, Hilde located a box and collected his personal effects from his office and desk. She glanced around and asked, "Anything else?"

He shook his head and finally seemed to wake from his state of shock. "Fräulein Dremmer, what am I supposed to do now?" he asked, fear and uncertainty on his face.

Hilde's heart went out to him. She knew he and his wife had three small children, the youngest one just two months old. With everything else going on in the country, he was unlikely to get a new job soon. What could she tell him?

"Herr Eppstein, I'm sorry, but maybe you should use this as an opportunity to get out of the country. See this as a silver lining and take your family someplace else." She lowered her voice. "Someplace safe."

"Where?" he asked brokenly, fighting back tears.

"How about Switzerland? The Swiss never get involved in these wars. There are lots of banks, and with your treasury experience, you should have no trouble finding a job."

Adam Eppstein gave her a sad smile and then shook his head. "I wish that were possible, but my oldest son just started school. He is the best in his class. It was difficult enough to find a school that would take him."

"I understand your concern for your family, but how will you feel when you can't feed them? Maybe uprooting them is the lesser evil in this situation."

As he closed the door to his office for the last time,

Hilde walked with him down the hallway. "Do you really want to stay in a country where they treat you like horse dung?"

"Fräulein Dremmer, this is my home. I was born here. My parents were born here, my wife and her parents...my children. I have nowhere else to go."

Chapter 14

Q visited his mother, Ingrid. He had avoided visiting her before his trip to Klosters and Paris because she had a way of knowing what went on in his head. Since he was a child, she'd always known when he lied or even when he'd attempted to avoid certain topics. And his intelligence work was definitely a topic he wanted to avoid. It was better if she knew nothing about it.

Today was no exception and his plan to only recount the skiing proportion of the trip failed miserably. Over a cup of freshly brewed coffee, she stared at him and asked, "What are you *not* telling me, son?"

"Mother, there's nothing else."

She squinted her eyes and responded, "You're touching your earlobe, Wilhelm. You do that when you try to hide something from me."

Why did he blush like a schoolboy? He was a grown man and didn't have to report to his mother anymore. But because he loved her dearly, he didn't want to lie to her. "Mother. You're right. But I can't tell you. It's better if you don't know."

She stared at him for several long moments, then seemed to come to some internal decision. "Don't get yourself into trouble, Wilhelm." She patted his hand and changed the topic. "What inventions are you currently working on?"

His mother didn't understand much of science, but she always showed interest in his research and even though he was sure she didn't understand most of what he explained, she always remembered the details and proudly told all of her friends about her genius son.

"I'm working on a new type of mist filter that can be built into the gas masks used by soldiers fighting on the front lines of a war."

"Haven't you done that already at the Auer-Gesellschaft?" She seemed surprised.

"Yes, Mother, but the commercial rights to those inventions belong to them, and I want to find a new and better solution that doesn't infringe on the patents I filed while I was an employee there. Then I can sell the rights to other companies and more persons, soldiers as well as civilians, can profit from an affordable gas mask." He didn't mention he would give the rights free of charge to his Russian friends.

"*Liebling*, do you really think there will be another war? Haven't we suffered enough in the Great War?"

"I sure hope there won't be another war, but that doesn't stop me from preparing for one."

They talked a while longer before he stood up and kissed his mother on the cheek. "I have to leave. Take care, Mother."

Back in Oranienburg, he found a letter from the police on his doorstep and tore it open with trembling fingers. Once he'd read the note, a sigh of relief left his lungs.

The letter stated the investigation against him, alleging espionage, had been closed for lack of evidence. They'd enclosed the confiscated article and even apologized for the inconvenience. At least from this quarter he was free and clear.

***

As autumn approached, Q became increasingly unhappy with his working environment. Working all on his own was fine and well, but not having a well-equipped laboratory was frustrating and hindered his research.

During one of the regular meetings with his friends, Otto said, "You seem unhappy, my friend."

"It's just that I'm sick and tired of working from my apartment. I need to get my hands on a fully-equipped laboratory."

Jakob laughed. "It's about time, don't you think?"

"Yes, you need a change of scenery," Leopold said and added, "I happen to have connections at the Biological Reich Institute for Agriculture and Forestry. Why don't I make a call and set up a meeting between you and the director?"

Hope fluttered in his chest. "You'd do that?"

"Sure, if you want."

Q thought for a moment before he replied, "I guess I'm ready to join the ranks of common employees again. I'd love to meet with your acquaintance. You're sure it's not a bother?"

"Come on, that's what friends are for. And with your reputation, they'd be the lucky ones to employ you."

"They probably have never heard of me..."

Jakob chuckled. "As always, you're being modest Q. Berlin is such a small place, I'm sure everyone working in the scientific world has heard of you or read one of your articles. You have such a good standing in the scientific community and your dissertation on nitrous oxide was widely recognized as an important contribution to the advancement of chemistry."

Q nodded, feeling more light-hearted at the prospect, "Okay. Okay. Thank you, Leopold. Meeting the director of the Biological Reich Institute sounds like a fine idea."

A few days later, Q met with the director, who unfortunately wasn't as excited as Q or his friends. "Doctor Quedlin, I have to tell you that the investigation involving you, alleging industrial spying, gives me some pause for concern."

Q couldn't hide his surprise. "How did you even come to hear about that? There was no evidence that I had done anything untoward. In fact, the accusations came from a woman who thought herself romantically inclined towards me. When I didn't return her affection, she fabricated those accusations out of revenge."

The director raised a brow. "Director Hoffmann from the Auer-Gesellschaft never mentioned that part. As for the accusations being false, do you have anything to back that up?"

Q had come prepared and pulled the letter stating the investigation had been closed for lack of evidence from his briefcase. "That letter is from the court."

The director read it from top to bottom before handing it back. "You are surely aware of the new political powers at work. I would hate to fall under any suspicion with them. Are you by chance a member of the NSDAP, the Nazi party?"

Q shook his head. "I am a member of no political party. I'm a scientist and have no interest in politics. Joining a party should be for people who are interested in working in politics."

"So, it's true then?" The director squinted his eyes and scrutinized Q's face.

"What's true?" Q asked.

"That you don't like the Nazis?"

For a split-second, Q's breath hitched in his lungs, but he schooled his face before the director could notice anything but mild surprise in his expression. In the future, he had to be more careful about sharing his true feelings for the Nazis. Because he didn't want to start a prospective working relation with a lie, he decided to go with a half-truth, hoping to delude the director. "I did not say that, and my not joining the NSDAP is in no ways an indication that I do not support them."

He paused, pondering whether that was enough. The director extended the silence for at least another thirty seconds before he smiled. "Very good, then. I can offer you a position as a freelancer. Would that be acceptable to you?"

Q stood up and shook the director's hand. "That would be fine."

On his way home, Q toyed with the idea of joining the Nazi party as a way of providing better cover for his actions. But his stomach clenched at the mere thought of it. It was one thing to lie by omission, but acting out a lie day in day out by joining the Nazi party? No, he wasn't made for acting and pretending.

Leopold visited him in the evening to ask about the interview. "How did it go?"

"I'm not sure," Q answered. "He called me on the investigation about industrial espionage and wouldn't employ me because I'm not a member of the Nazi party. But he offered me a freelancer job instead."

"That sucks. And I understand how you feel. The government has already suggested I give preference to party members for jobs overseeing the research and development area for my company."

Q pursed his lips and shrugged.

"Look at it this way, being a freelancer is much better than being on staff. You will have more control of your schedule and can travel and do research on your own without permission."

"And I will have that great big laboratory at my disposal. I haven't worked with plant care and protection, but I'm excited about this new area of study."

"I'm sure you'll do fine."

"I just hope this new kind of work won't be used for military purposes. I'm sick and tired of having my inventions used to militarize a country instead of serving the human race and the goal of peace."

Most of his later work at Auer-Gesellschaft had been geared toward military usage, and his inventions had been exploited for use against other human beings.

Like his work with the arsenic compounds and other gases. He'd seen the reports and heard the rumors. Instead of using his discoveries to protect people, they were now being twisted and used to kill via gasification. It sickened him to know he'd been a part in making those weapons possible.

"Plant protection will keep you out of the military focus," Leopold said.

"Let's hope so, by goodness. Because I'm fairly certain Hitler's ultimate goal is world domination which will push Germany into another war, even more destructive than the last one. And I don't want to be part of that!"

Leopold tried to calm down his friend. "Q, you're so pessimistic. People learned their lessons from the last war and they won't repeat the past. You just have to trust them. The Great War was the war to end all wars."

Q shook his head. "I'm not so sure about that. Communism is the only form of government able to provide a peaceful co-existence of all nations because the core value of communism is the philosophy that all humans are created equal."

Leopold laughed at his naïve take on communism. "Where on earth did you get that idea?"

Q frowned. "*Decline of the West* by Oswald Spengler."

Leopold merely grinned at him and asked, "So, you've never actually read the theories about communism and Marxism?"

"No."

"Then you should. I think you might be in for a surprise."

"Why is that?" Q asked, not really paying attention to the discussion anymore. He knew what he knew. Leopold or reading some books wouldn't change that.

"Because your idealized version of communism doesn't exist. It's not the way you think it is."

Q shook his head. "I know enough." In his scientific mind, communism sounded perfect. All humans were created as equals. Everyone working for the best of the community. One for all and all for one. "I don't need to read about Marxism. Those are just political theories. I have important scientific research to do."

Leopold raised a brow and shook his head. "You should make time."

That statement continued to roll around in his head, long after he and Leopold parted ways. Had he gotten it all wrong?

No, not him.

Chapter 15

Spring came to 1934 and things in Germany had slowly deteriorated, but Q had managed to carve out an existence he could live with. At least for the time being.

A few weeks ago, he'd left his flat in Oranienburg with the nosy landlady to move into a slightly bigger two-bedroom flat in the center of Berlin that suited his bachelor needs quite nicely. Partly nostalgic and partly satisfied to turn over a new leaf in his life, he also stopped subletting the room at Jakob's place.

One evening in April, he and Leopold headed to the movies. With the current political situation creating stress for everyone, they needed a distraction. Stan Laurel and Oliver Hardy, commonly referred to as "*Dick und Doof*" had released a new short film, *Going Bye-Bye*. Their slapstick comedy was the perfect way to end a week of hard work, at least in Q's opinion.

Leopold wasn't as fond of their humor but tagged along because he'd get to choose the next movie. They sat in the dark theater and Q elbowed Leopold several times because he kept quiet during some of the most hilarious scenes. "Come on, this is funny."

His friend growled. "Kinda."

During the first reel, a group of women a few rows in front of them caught his attention because one of them laughed loudly at every punchline, even when everyone else didn't seem to get it.

Q couldn't make out which of the three girls it was, but her sense of humor and her unconcerned laughter intrigued him. For some reason, this unknown woman sparked his interest, and he hadn't actually seen her yet.

This attraction puzzled him. He hadn't been this intrigued by a woman in – ever. Sure, he'd gone out with a few, but sooner or later, he'd always become bored and preferred to dedicate his time to his research than to a woman. His friends had begun teasing him about how he was married to science and might as well become a Catholic priest. And their teasing had only intensified now that he'd turned thirty-one. All of his friends were happily married or at least engaged at this age.

I don't need a woman to be happy. She'll only distract me from my inventions. She'd never understand.

But when he saw the three girls standing in the vast lobby of the theater during the small fifteen-minute break between reels, he couldn't resist approaching them. The three of them looked like a commercial for German gals: sandy, dark blonde, and brunette. All of them with bright blue eyes and the sandy blonde wore her hair in traditional pretzel braids.

Then she spoke, and the sound of her soft feminine voice drew him near like a siren. When he finally distinguished her, he had to swallow back a lump in his throat. *Oh my god, she's so beautiful.* Her dark blonde hair fell in soft waves around her shoulders and against her neck. She had it tied back with a ribbon, and he wondered if it was as soft as it looked.

His eyes wandered down her body, and he was

struck by her appearance. Instead of wearing a dress and stockings like most of the other girls, she clothed herself in a short-sleeved white blouse and long, wide legged pants. She stood proudly, her back straight and he was reminded of a picture of Marlene Dietrich in a similar pose.

While he'd never seen the actress in person, he admired her for her strong character, the way she always said what she thought, and her audacity in wearing pantsuits in public. No woman had ever dared to that before. Except maybe for the beauty standing in front of him.

"Good evening, ladies. May we join you for a moment?"

When they nodded in unison, suppressing their giggles, he continued, "I'm Wilhelm Quedlin, but my friends call me Q. This is my friend Leopold Stieber."

He watched the blonde blush as she introduced herself. "Good evening. I'm Hildegard Dremmer, but my friends call me Hilde. These are my friends Erika and Gertrud."

While Leopold engaged in small talk with her girlfriends, Q took a step closer to Hilde and complimented her on her choice of attire. "You look like Marlene Dietrich in that outfit."

She flashed the cutest blush. "You think so?"

"I do. But I like the color of your hair much better."

"Hmm, thanks," was all she said.

Q was enthralled with the way Hilde seemed tongue-tied around him. She kept glancing up at him from beneath her long dark lashes, and when she spoke to him, she sounded almost out of breath. He wanted nothing more than to touch her silky hair, but that would, of course, be inappropriate. Instead, he said, "I noticed how much you laughed at *Dick und Doof*, they're my favorite actors."

She blushed a shade darker. "Ahem...yes...was I laughing too loud?"

By any normal standard, her laughter had been way too loud, but he shook his head. "Not at all. I loved it. It's a rare occasion to hear someone laugh unconcerned in these days."

A shadow crossed her face before she nodded. "Times are difficult, aren't they?"

Q had no intention to go down the sorry road of the overall economic and political situation in Germany and looked for a better topic to discuss when the first bell interrupted his train of thought. They'd have to go inside the theater in a minute, and this was maybe his only chance. "Would you allow me to invite you for afternoon coffee one day?"

She side-glanced at her friends before answering, "I'd love to."

Q's heart jumped, and he smiled at her. "Perfect. How about next Saturday? Three p.m. at the Café Potsdamer Platz?"

Hilde nodded. "Yes."

Moments later, the bell rang again and the lights dimmed, indicating the second reel was loaded and ready to begin. Q took Hilde's hand and kissed the back of it. "Until next Saturday, beautiful. I shall meet you at Potsdamer Platz."

Leopold stood next to him and watched Hilde and her girlfriends disappear inside. "You do realize she's much too young for an old man like you?"

Q tore his eyes away from the girl who'd conquered him like a whirlwind and looked straight into the face of his friend. "No. She's just right."

"Come on, she can't be much older than twenty."

"Twenty-two. I asked." Q grinned at him. "Leopold, congratulate me."

"On what? Robbing the cradle?"

"No. You've just been the first person to meet my future wife."

Chapter 16

Hilde returned to the movie theater with Erika and Gertrude, but her mind wasn't on the second half of the film. It was on the handsome stranger who'd just asked her out. Q was tall and slim, and even though his blond hair had been cut very short, she believed it would be curly if left to grow.

His narrow, long face featured a very pronounced chin and dark eyebrows behind his rimless glasses. She actually liked the glasses, they gave him a very intellectual look. And the way he spoke showed he was a man of education. Maybe a teacher? She cursed herself for not asking some questions about him. Like what he did for a living. She'd have to ask more questions when they met again.

Next Saturday! Part of her already longed to see him again, to get to know him better, but another part of her was horribly scared and made plans to balk.

Her heart was still beating faster, and she hoped she hadn't made a complete fool of herself while he flirted with her. Apparently, he hadn't been completely deterred by her tongue-tied behavior because he'd asked her out. And she was still shocked that she'd agreed. *Haven't you vowed to never fall in love? This man has the power to hurt you.*

After the movie ended, Erika and Gertrud started their inquisition. "I can't believe you agreed to go out with that man. You don't even know him," Erika said while they left the building.

"He's not exactly the type who'd make the cover of a magazine. And he wears glasses," Gertrud added.

"The glasses give him a serene and intellectual look. I liked it." Hilde tried to defend her admirer.

"You can't be serious. And he was so skinny. He probably doesn't exercise ever."

Hilde heard her friends tearing Q apart, but she let their comments flow over her. "What's wrong with tall and slim? I don't need a muscle man. I want someone I can look up to. An intelligent man."

"Where does he work?" Gertrud asked as they rounded the corner.

"Probably a teacher. He has that look about him," Erika surmised.

"No way. He's not that smart. He's probably a clerk in a clothing store or something boring like that."

"How old do you think he is?" Erika asked Gertrud as if Hilde wasn't present.

"Too old for Hilde to be going out with him."

Hilde made a face at them. "Maybe for you, but I think he's just right. Not like those silly boys our age." Behind his serious appearance, she'd spotted a hidden glint of mischief in his amazing blue eyes. No, he wasn't some dreadfully boring clerk. She could feel it. His eyes had captured her with their meaningfulness. And a man whose favorite actors were Stan and Ollie must have a sense of humor.

As they passed their favorite diner, Hilde asked, "Girls, want a soda before we head home?"

"Sure, but I have to be back before midnight," Erika reminded her.

"Me too. Say, does your mother never give you a curfew?" Gertrud asked.

Hilde shrugged. "No."

Her mother didn't care what time she came home each night. One of the reasons she'd moved to Berlin had been to get away from her over-protective father and stepmother. So why did she feel stabbed in her heart every time her friends complained about their well-meaning and concerned parents? *I should be happy about my freedom. Wasn't that what I wanted?*

She pushed those thoughts aside before hurt and guilt could settle in her soul. Thinking about how she'd left her father after that terrible fight was the surest way to ruin the evening.

As they entered the small diner and placed their orders, she turned her thoughts away from her parents and back to the man who called himself Q. *Now, he's worth thinking about.*

Chapter 17

Q looked forward to meeting the beautiful Hilde again all week long. In fact, she occupied so much space in his brain, he even made a mistake in one of his calculations and ended up having to throw away two days of work to start the experiment again.

That was such an unusual behavior for him that he almost decided to forget about her. She was becoming the thing he feared. A distraction.

But after giving it some consideration, he found she intrigued him enough to risk his focus to meet with her. Apart from her obvious beauty, it was more than her looks that drew him to her. The way she dressed and the self-confidence she exuded made him want to get to know the woman underneath.

He sensed she owned an inner strength that was at odds with the way she'd been so tongue-tied at their last meeting. Her shyness had been cute, but he wondered how the real Hilde would behave.

Saturday arrived, and Q made sure to arrive with plenty of time to spare. He parked his car where several roads converged at the big public square in the center of Berlin. Entering the square from the south, he passed the Brandenburg Gate and the Reichstag building, which had been in flames one year before, causing the government to basically suspend the basic human rights granted in the *Weimarer Verfassung*.

Q watched the Reichstag and fought down a bitter

taste, while he recited a verse from *The Sorcerer's Apprentice* by Johann Wolfgang von Goethe:

Sir, my need is sore.

Spirits that I've cited

My commands ignore.

People would soon find out that this was only the first of many stages leading Germany straight into a National Socialist dictatorship. Hopefully, it wouldn't be too late by then.

Hilde arrived at the Café Potsdamer Platz a few minutes later from the north. He spotted her buoyant stride long before he could distinguish her face and met her halfway, greeting her with a huge grin. *"Guten Tag. How are you, lovely Hilde, on this wonderful afternoon?"*

Her cheeks stained with a deep purple blush, and she cast her eyes down as she answered, "I'm fine, thank you."

Q mused about her adorable shyness and decided to redeem her. "Would you like to get something to drink or eat?"

"How about we have some coffee and possibly a pastry?" she suggested.

Q led her towards one of the tables in the outdoor area, and they placed their order with the waitress. "I've been looking forward to meeting you, Hilde. Tell me something about you. Do you work?"

She gave him an indignant look. "Of course I work. I finished business school several years ago and was lucky to get a job processing client claims for an insurance company."

So she doesn't buy into the Nazi ideology of being solely a housewife and mother. "Were you born in Berlin?" he asked, sipping his coffee as it arrived.

"No, I was born in Hamburg. I lived there until I was eighteen and then I moved here to live with my mother, step-father, and half-brother."

Q nodded and tabled his questions for later because her voice clearly indicated she didn't wish to talk about her family. "Well, I'm glad you moved to Berlin. Otherwise, I would have missed meeting the most beautiful woman in the world."

Hilde blushed and dedicated her attention to her fingernails. When Q watched her in silence, she soon regained her composure and raised her head. He looked into the most beautiful blue eyes he'd ever seen, and his heart warmed.

"So what about you?" she asked.

Q trailed a finger down her hand that lay on the table top. "I was born in Magdeburg. My parents moved to Berlin when I was fifteen, and I, naturally, came with them."

"So, what do you do for a living?" she asked, her eyes dilating with what he hoped was excitement when he slipped her fingers into his hand.

"I'm a scientist. I studied chemistry at university and have a PhD in engineering. Right now, I'm working for the Biological Reich Institute of Agriculture and Forestry as a freelancer."

"That sounds very interesting." She glanced at him with the sweetest expression and his heart melted.

"It is, but working with plants is not my passion."

"What is?" she asked, and he became acutely aware of her warm, soft fingers in his hand.

"Research. Inventions. Making discoveries that can be used for the good of mankind."

"Like what?" Her eyes lit up with genuine interest, and he felt encouraged to tell her about his passion. Not a single woman he'd gone out with had ever wanted to know more about his inventions. But Hilde did.

He recounted some of his findings, and soon their discussion turned into a light-hearted banter, where they discovered each other's likes and dislikes. Q enjoyed the conversation and time flew by. Both of them looked surprised when the waitress politely informed them several hours later that the Café was about to close.

"Can I drive you home?"

"That would be nice."

Q walked by her side, leading the way to his automobile, and after going several yards, he reached over and took her hand in his own. He opened the door for her, and she gave him directions to her house. Once there, he asked, "Can I ask you out again?"

Hilde nodded. "I would like that."

"Me too. I had such a wonderful time today."

"So did I." She led him up to the front door of the five-story apartment building, suddenly acting more nervous than she had all day long.

Q watched her carefully, trying to decide whether he

should kiss her or not. He really wanted to, but her nervousness had him deciding to place a brief kiss on her cheek. When he pulled away, he was glad for his decision. She seemed distraught, biting her bottom lip.

Moments later, he walked away, feeling happier than he could remember. *She's definitely going to be my wife.*

Chapter 18

A few days later, Q picked her up from her place of work and took her out to dinner at a local restaurant. It was a lovely spring evening, and they were able to sit outside at a table near the back of the garden area.

The nicely arranged garden with lush green bushes and beautiful flower beds boasting pink peonies, blue clematis, and white lily of the valley, smelled of the coming summer and lightheartedness. A feeling so many citizens of Berlin had almost forgotten existed.

Hilde was clearly as enchanted by the peaceful surroundings as he was and they relaxed into their seats, enjoying their dinner and each other's company. When a flower girl came by their table, he purchased a red rose for Hilde, smelling it before handing it to her with a wink. "For you, my dear."

"Thank you," she said as she took the rose and touched his hand in a caring gesture.

Q watched her for a moment and on an impulse, he asked, "Would you like to come with me to visit my brother Gunther? He lives in a small town about two hours from Berlin by car. You'll love the peaceful atmosphere there."

"Now?" she asked with a twinkle in her eyes.

"Of course not." He grinned. "In two or three weeks from now. We'll leave early on a Sunday morning. Make a full day of it."

She made a face as if she was pondering his question before she burst out laughing. "I'd love to."

Q smiled back and thought what a lucky man he was. Later, he escorted her from the restaurant and drove her home. He walked her up to the doorstep, and this time, he didn't hesitate to kiss her. They shared a passionate kiss and were still locked in one another's arms when the sound of a female chuckle came from behind them.

He quickly released Hilde and stepped away, watching the older woman as she came forward and eyed him with blue eyes so similar to Hilde's. "Don't stop on my account."

Hilde was clearly embarrassed as he could see by the chagrin on her face. He stepped in front of her and addressed the woman. "Good Evening. I'm sorry for the disturbance. My name is Wilhelm Quedlin."

"I'm Marianne, Hilde's mother." She started to unlock the door and then turned back and noticed his black Ford sitting on the curb. "You came here by automobile?"

Q nodded and wanted to leave, but Marianne touched his arm. "Why don't you come on in, Wilhelm?" she asked before turning to her daughter. "Hilde, no need to keep your beau outside."

She led the way into the staircase and up to the third floor. Q followed her, not exactly sure what to think. He'd expected Hilde's mother to reprimand him for kissing her daughter on the doorstep, but inviting him in? That was pretty unusual.

Marianne unlocked the apartment door and seated

him on the big couch in the tiny living room, and Q took a look around. It was sparsely furnished. An antique wooden bureau adorned the wall opposite the sofa and to the left was a beautiful cupboard holding the good china. The centerpiece of the room was a glass coffee table surrounded by a dark leather couch and two matching chairs. Every piece was of timeless beauty. Hilde's mother obviously had good, and expensive, taste.

When Hilde went to sit down at the far end of the couch, her mother tsked at her. "Go sit next to your man. For goodness sake, he's going to think you're a prude."

Q looked from mother to daughter, feeling the tension between them and it dawned on him why Hilde never wanted to talk about her family. It was so different from the way he and his mother treated each other.

Hilde reluctantly moved closer to him, careful to leave enough space between them to avoid any accidental touch. Her awkwardness was visible on her face, and he could sense it in the tension she emitted.

Her mother didn't seem to notice. "It's so lovely to have you here, Wilhelm. Hilde hasn't talked much about you. Tell me, what is it you do for a living?"

"I'm a scientist."

"Oh, how interesting. You're a professor at the university?"

"Not quite. I work at the Biological Reich Institute for Agriculture and Forestry in the field of plant protection."

"You work for the government. Now that is promising. Tell me more."

"The Reich Institute is funded by the state, but we're not actually working for the government. We're an independent scientific institution." *At least for the time being.*

Marianne went on to ask questions about his background, his automobile, his flat and he couldn't help but compare his current situation with the interview he'd had with the bank clerk when he'd applied for the loan. Biting back a laugh, he waited for her to ask to see his bank account statements.

But one look at Hilde's agonized expression sobered him up. "It's been a lovely discussion, *Gnädige Frau* but I should probably head home now."

"Nonsense, and please call me Annie." She looked at her daughter. "Wilhelm can come by whenever he wants. He-"

"Annie," Q interrupted and stood up, "I'm very thankful for your generous welcome, but I'm afraid I have to get up very early tomorrow morning and should bid goodbye."

Hilde's mother stretched out her hand, "I hope to see you again soon. And don't worry about bringing my daughter home late. I won't even mind if you drop her off in the morning."

Startled, he looked down at Hilde, who was looking down at her wringing hands. "I'll see you on Saturday, my dear."

Q left the apartment and walked back to his car, trying to process what Annie had said. He'd never been in such a strange situation. *Did she just invite me to sleep with her daughter? What kind of weird, twisted relationship is this?*

***

Hilde wished the floor would open up and swallow her whole. Q hadn't shown any sign of annoyance, considering her mother had been almost vulgar. But then again, Q was always nice to everyone, regardless who they were.

But now he probably wouldn't want to see her ever again. She hid her face behind her hands and wanted to scream.

When her mother returned from walking Q to the door, Hilde couldn't take it anymore and shouted at her, "What was that all about? Do you want him to believe I'm a tramp?"

Annie waved away her daughter's concern. "Oh, don't be that way. That's what young people do. You should be enjoying life."

Hilde shook her head in disgust. She wasn't fooled at all by her mother's acceptance of Q. The minute she'd seen his automobile parked at the curb, Hilde had seen the dollar signs in her mother's eyes. "You're unbelievable. The only reason you like him is because you think he has money."

"Well, doesn't he?"

"Maybe or maybe not. I don't care." Hilde fought the urge to grab her mother by the neck and shake her until her brains rattled.

"You should," her mother said, straightening the

pillows on the couch.

"You're always looking out for yourself."

"What's wrong with that? When you're older, you will understand having a husband to provide for you is important. And in these troubling times, it's doubly important that he has enough money and a safe job."

"I don't need a man to take care of me." Hilde stomped her foot.

"Whoever put those silly ideas in your head, it wasn't me. I tried to teach you the right things. A good woman stays at home and raises her children. She does the laundry, has a warm meal on the table for her husband when he comes home from work, and makes sure her children behave in a way she and the *Führer* can be proud of."

"And what if that isn't the life I want? What if I want to provide for myself?" Hilde growled, her eyes squinting in fury.

Annie raised her head for a moment to look at her daughter before she busied herself dusting the coffee table. "My dear daughter, you need to start paying attention. This is what we women are meant to do. It doesn't do you any good to rebel against God and your Fatherland."

Hilde opened up her mouth to respond, but her mother bulldozed over her.

"In this dire economy, everyone has to make a sacrifice, and when good men are out of work, it's selfish and anti-German for a married woman not to voluntarily give up her job so a man can work and provide for his family."

Hilde had heard of women being fired from their jobs for exactly that reason. She knew everything about the Nazi ideal of a "good German woman" and she disagreed with almost every single point of it. "I want to be free and independent. But you wouldn't understand that, would you, Mother? You haven't worked a single day in your entire life."

"You don't know how difficult raising two children is," her mother answered.

It was the first time she acted this rude against her mother, and while she knew she was crossing the line, she couldn't hold back anymore. The bottled up emotions of twenty years had reached the boiling point, and the words left her mouth like an explosion.

"Raising children? I don't remember you being around when I was young. You didn't raise me; you never even loved me! You dumped me off at Granny's house to go traipsing around with your new lover. And I seriously doubt you had much to do with raising my half-brother."

"You ungrateful little tramp!"

Hilde caught her breath and stared her mother down before she stalked towards her bedroom. "That's right. I'm ungrateful. I don't appreciate how you abandoned your two-year old daughter while my father was at war. I'd rather be ungrateful, thank you very much."

She slammed the door to the bedroom and sank down onto the bed in desolation. But instead of the tears she'd expected, her eyes stayed dry, and a sense of relief washed over her. There, she'd said it. She'd told her mother how much she'd suffered from being abandoned as a child.

Chapter 19

Hilde was early for work because she'd hurried out of the house, wanting to avoid her mother. The entrance door was still closed, so she took off for a walk around the block. Her eyes cast to the ground, her shoulders hunched, she shuffled along and shrieked when she bumped into someone and felt herself embraced by two strong arms.

"I called out to you, but you were in your own world," Q's familiar voice said before he pressed a kiss on her lips.

She gave in to his kiss and let him hold her a few moments longer before she broke free and straightened her summer dress. "You still want to see me?"

"Why wouldn't I want to see you, sweetest of all women?" he asked, stroking a finger down her cheek.

"Because, you know, yesterday…my mother…she was… I mean…"

He took her chin into his hands and gently forced her to look at him. "*Liebste,* Hilde. I will only judge you on your own actions, never on those of other persons. So, do we still meet on Saturday?"

She nodded and sent him a happy smile. "Thanks for coming. I was worried you'd never want to see me again."

"I know. That's why I came to look for you. Now let me walk you to your work. You wouldn't want to give them a reason to fire you, right?"

***

Three weeks later, Hilde and Q were officially going together item and were seeing each other almost every other day. As promised, they drove out of Berlin to visit his brother Gunther and his family in a small village by the Baltic.

"Tell me about your brother's family," she said as she watched him drive and thought how lucky she was to have a man like him in her life.

"Gunther has been married to a wonderful woman named Katrin for twenty years, and they have four children. The youngest is nine years old."

"Twenty years? How old is he?"

Q chuckled before he answered. "He's ancient. Fifteen years older than me."

"That explains a lot. What does he do?" she asked while looking out the window. They had left the city of Berlin behind and drove now through the countryside. Fewer and fewer buildings lined the street and gave way to vast open areas with wheat and potato fields.

"He's a lawyer."

"Oh," Hilde murmured.

"Yes, oh. So, how was your work?"

"Boring."

"And your mother?"

Hilde made a face at him. "You know perfectly well

that I don't want to discuss my mother."

Q chuckled. "Yes, I know."

"I'm thinking about moving out. She probably wouldn't even notice."

He glanced at her for a moment and reached over to take her hand. "If I can help you with anything, let me know. Just don't get into too big of a hurry."

"I won't. How do you do it?" she asked.

"Do what?"

"Whenever I'm with you, I feel so safe and…loved. Being with you is comfortable and never awkward."

"Never?" he asked with a mischievous grin that told her he was thinking back to their first couple of dates when she hadn't done much more than blushed and mumbled.

"Well, maybe the first couple of times we went out, but not now. You accept me just as I am, and you let me speak my mind."

"That's because it's such a beautiful mind," he lifted their joined hands and kissed the back of hers.

Hilde settled back into the seat, enjoying the ride in the small black Ford. "Q, this trip was a good idea."

"I'm an inventor. Having good ideas is my job."

She giggled. "I'll try to remember next time."

After driving a while in silence, she asked him, "Why doesn't your brother live in Berlin. Wouldn't there be more work for a lawyer?"

"That's a long story."

"I'm all ears."

He squeezed her fingers and seemed to think about his words. "Gunther worked as head of the department in the education ministry in Berlin, where he was responsible for the legal affairs of all German State Universities – until the Nazi's suspended him almost one year ago."

She glanced over at Q's seemingly calm face. "But why? Did he do anything wrong?"

Q coughed out a bitter laugh. "The only wrong he did was to be a registered member of the Social Democratic Party. They suspended him because he wouldn't cancel his party membership and join the Nazi party NSDAP. He was suspended, and a short time later, they forced him to retire with a minimal pension at the age of forty-six."

"I'm so sorry."

"Yes, me too. Without a job and four kids to provide for he had to move out here because the costs of living in Berlin were just too high."

"Couldn't he get a new job?" she asked.

"He never took the final exams required to work as a lawyer at court. As far as I know, he's done that now and is waiting for approval from some ministry to be admitted as a lawyer."

Hilde clenched her fists and wanted to punch someone. How could Q stay so calm witnessing this kind of injustice? She shouted out, "The Nazis have ruined so many things for so many people. I hate them!"

Q reached over and squeezed her hand. "Hilde you

mustn't ever say those things in public. It's not safe."

"Last time I checked, we still had freedom of speech," she said through gritted teeth.

Without Hilde noticing, Q had stopped the car at the curb and turned towards her. "Hildelein, it's not safe. One wrong word might get you into trouble nowadays. You never know whom you can trust."

The concern on his face was so intense, her heart squeezed. *He must know a lot more about the current situation than I do.* She sighed. "I wish everyone would shout out their hate from the top of their lungs. As loud as they can."

"I wish that too sometimes, but the time isn't right. The Nazis have eyes and ears everywhere. It's better to blend in and not fall under any suspicion than to have them openly watching you."

"I hate them," she repeated like a stubborn little girl. "How can I pretend to like them? Since I was small, I've started discussions and fights about things I thought wrong."

"You'll have to change. You're an adult now. You can do that."

"I guess I can." She sighed, deep and loud.

Q squeezed her hand a bit harder. "I don't want anything bad happening to you," he said, his voice hard and demanding, his eyes piercing into hers. "Promise me!"

His genuine concern for her safety warmed her heart. If this was how it felt to be loved, then maybe she should reconsider her vow not to love anymore? She leaned over to kiss him on the cheek. "I promise. I'll keep all of my hate speech about the Nazi's for your ears alone."

Q tapped her nose. "Thank you. I look forward to hearing it."

He started the engine again and headed towards their destination. As they entered the small town where Gunther lived, Hilde had the strange feeling something was missing. But what?

It took her a few moments to realize that this cute little town looked like in the old days.

No sign of the Nazi reign.

No uniformed SA or SS patrolled the streets.

No Nazi flags hung from prominent buildings, probably for the lack of ostentatious buildings.

They passed a few people, and her mouth hung open when Q waved a greeting, and the people waved back.

"Close your mouth, Hilde. You'll catch flies."

She snapped it closed, then opened it again to say, "They waved at you and smiled."

"Yes. Feels good, doesn't it?"

"This is so different than Berlin. It seems like a different planet. Nice and quiet."

"It is." He parked the car in front of a modest two-story red-brick family home. "We've arrived."

Chapter 20

Gunther opened the door and rushed out, hugging Q and giving Hilde a handshake. "Welcome in my modest exile."

Q clapped him on the back. "Good to see you. Where's Katrin?"

"She left yesterday evening with the kids to visit her parents. Her mother is very sick."

"Maybe next time," Q suggested and followed his brother inside the house. He recognized the furniture in the hall and living room from his brother's former flat in Berlin. They showed the wear of four children having mistreated them, and for a moment, the image of Hilde's and his children climbing over the sofa and chasing each other around the coffee table flashed through his mind. He grabbed her hand and couldn't hide his huge smile.

Gunther asked them to wait in the living room while he prepared coffee and served the cake Katrin had baked for their guests. When they'd settled around the table and sipped their coffee, Hilde complimented Gunther on the beautiful garden and the cute little house.

"It's nice, yes, but we might move back to Berlin soon."

"How's that?" Q asked.

"I took the missing exam and received approval by

the court of first instance to start working as a lawyer."

"They approved you? Just like that?" Q asked. "When the Nazis dismissed you from your role in the education ministry, I feared they wouldn't approve you as a common lawyer either."

Gunther gave his brother a tight smile with a side-glance at Hilde. "Even the current government sees the need for competent lawyers."

"Yes," Q agreed. "But wouldn't you be working for Nazis? I know you hate them and what they stand for."

"I may not agree with everything our current government does, but as an attorney, my sole guidance is the law, which is the same for everyone." He eyed Hilde with a suspicious look that clearly conveyed that Q was speaking too much.

Laughing, Q nodded in her direction. "Don't worry, brother. She's trustworthy."

"How can you be so sure?" Gunther asked.

"I know her."

"You just can't be too sure these days. I don't know whom to trust right now."

Gunther glared at them, and Q felt the need to defend Hilde. He could understand where his brother came from, but it had to stop where his girlfriend was concerned. "Well, you trust me, and I trust Hilde. That must be enough."

"But what do you really know about her? Or her parents for that matter? Isn't her step-father the celebrated opera singer Robert Klein?"

"Yes, he is. I haven't met him though."

Gunther snorted rudely. "For heaven's sake! He's still on the stage performing."

"So what?"

"Q, you know as well as I do that every artist who has in any form criticized the regime has been punished with stage ban. If he's still performing, he must be a supporter of the Nazis."

"Maybe. Or maybe he's just part of the silent majority. Keeping his mouth shut to hold on to his job? And what does that have to do with Hilde?"

"Like father like son."

"Gunther, you're being unfair. He's her step-father."

"She lives with them, doesn't she? You can't trust her. What if she says the wrong thing and they turn her in? Or you? Or me?"

Q was getting annoyed at his brother. Gunther could be so bullheaded. He wanted to give a sharp response when Hilde raised her voice. "Excuse me, but I'm sitting right here. There is no need to talk about me as if I weren't."

She glared at Gunther. "You don't have to trust me, but believe me when I tell you I hate the Nazis and everything they stand for."

"Why? What did they do to you? What do your parents believe?" Gunther fired one question after another without giving Hilde time to answer. "What is your political conviction? Are you an NSDAP member? Are your parents? What are their loyalties?"

Hilde shook her head and finally interrupted him. "I'm not a member of any party, and I don't know whether my mother or Robert are. Politics was never a topic of discussion at either my father's or my mother's house."

"And yet you want me to believe you hate the Nazis and wouldn't go off denouncing anyone at the first chance you get?" he said with a derisive grin.

"I do."

"If politics were never discussed at your home, how do you know anything about it? What have the Nazis done to you that justifies your hatred?"

"Nothing. But I could ask you the same questions."

Gunther gave a harsh laugh. "They fired me, and that's enough for me."

Hilde jumped up, and Q put a calming hand on her leg, urging her to sit down again. "Why don't we just agree that none of us here like the Nazis and talk about something else? The weather? Or the peaceful town?"

Gunther and Hilde stared at each other like two boxers in the ring, but then Hilde relaxed and said, "Truce?"

"Truce," Gunther agreed, the smile not quite reaching his eyes.

Their visit didn't last much longer, and they soon sat in his Ford returning home. Hilde had become quiet after arguing with his brother, and he was worried about her. "I'm sorry. He's not usually like that."

Hilde didn't hold back. "I don't like him at all. He's unfair and self-righteous. He honestly thinks he's the only one entitled to hate the Nazis."

"Yes, he does, but keep in mind he is a good man. I

know he doesn't come across very friendly, but he's changed during the last year. Losing his prestigious job and having to move his family away from Berlin has left so much bitterness and hurt in his soul. But he'll come around. You two will get along better the more you get to know him."

"Do you have any more brothers or sisters?" she asked after a while.

Instead of answering her right away, he fixated his eyes on the street and grew very quiet. Even though she had to see how his knuckles turned white grabbing the steering wheel, she didn't pressure him, just waited patiently for him to speak. *That's why I love her so much.* His voice was shaky when he finally answered her question.

"I'm the youngest of four brothers. You just met Gunther, the oldest. He's fifteen years my senior. Then came Knut and Albert, thirteen and eleven years older than me."

"You were the baby of the family," she said with a teasing tone. "The nestling. Not like me, I'm the oldest sibling."

He kept quiet, hoping she'd let go of the topic, but no such luck.

"When will I get to meet your other brothers?"

Q debated not answering her. Talking about his family always dredged up bad memories.

"Q?" she asked, concern evident in her voice, "You don't have to tell me if you don't want to."

He glanced at her, and his heart softened at the view of her sweet face. It wasn't right to keep this part of his story from her. She was the woman he wanted to spend the rest of his life with, and she had a right to know. He shook his head. "No. They are dead."

She blew out a breath and reached for his hand. "I'm sorry. What happened?"

He gripped the steering wheel even harder. "Albert was a very intelligent young man. A mathematician. Some called him brilliant. During the last war, he joined up, even though his profession was exempt. He wanted to do his duty, serve his country. You know, all this stupid talk about national honor? Well, he became a pilot and went down over France."

"How awful." She slapped a hand over her mouth and for a tiny moment, she thought about her father and how grateful she was that he had made it back alive from the frontlines of the Great War.

"Yes. It was. He was shot down. Other planes in the area didn't see him get out. According to their eyewitness reports, his plane nosedived into the ground and exploded. He must have died instantly."

"I'm very sorry."

"Life wasn't the same after we got the notice. Albert had just turned twenty-three and had a beautiful girlfriend waiting for him at home. It was a horrible waste of a young and promising life. I was ten back then, and he'd been my hero since I can remember." Q paused for a moment and then murmured, "This is why I hate war so much. It takes so many lives – causes so much grief. We humans should be wiser than to start another war."

Hilde left him alone with his thoughts for a while

before she asked in a soft voice, "And your other brother? Knut?"

Q sighed. "We don't know. He disappeared in Norway."

"Disappeared? I don't understand."

He gave her a rueful smile. "Neither does my mother. Knut was an adventurer. He was always on the move, traveling somewhere. Exploring, he called it. He never contented himself going the beaten path. No, he always had to go where nobody else had been before. Since he left for his trip to Norway five years ago, we haven't heard from him again."

"Oh, the not knowing…" she trailed off.

He nodded. "My mother, Ingrid, still holds out hope that one day he will show up on her doorstep with a bag full of stories to tell. But Gunther and I are almost certain he's dead."

He could see Hilde was fighting tears when she talked again. "That must be horrible for your mother. I mean, losing a child is probably the worst thing that can happen to you. But the insecurity, not knowing for certain your son is indeed dead and not knowing if he needs your help…that is even worse."

Q nodded. "1929 was a very hard year for my family. Knut went missing, and a few weeks later, my father died unexpectedly from the aftermath of pneumonia. He was showing signs of recovery when, overnight, an embolism in his lung finished him off."

"Your poor mother," Hilde murmured. "Does she live in Berlin?"

"Yes." Q was quiet for a while and then added.

"Now, maybe you can understand why Gunther was so harsh about talking in front of you. Neither my brother nor myself have any intentions of adding to the list of deceased children. My mother has had enough sorrow in her life."

Q let his thoughts drift to his missing brother. It had been so long. Knut definitely had his flaws, but he wouldn't just disappear without trying to get some kind of word to his mother that he was well and alive. Knut was dead.

This conversation was a good reminder that he needed to take more precautions about his intelligence work for the Russians. He didn't want to give the German authorities any reason to look in his direction. His mother shouldn't have to lose another son.

Chapter 21

Hilde enjoyed the drive back to Berlin until Q turned the tables and asked about her family. She made a face at him, but he insisted, "Now that I've told you my sad story, it's only fair you do the same."

"Well, I live with my mother, whom you've had the misfortune to meet."

Q chuckled "She is…different."

"You could definitely say that. All my girlfriends envy me because she's so laid back and never gives me a curfew or opposes my choice of clothing, but sometimes I'd rather…"

"…fight with her about how long you're allowed to stay out?" He completed her sentence.

Now that he'd voiced it, it sounded strange, and she had to laugh. "I know, it sounds strange, but sometimes I think she doesn't care about me. She probably wouldn't even notice if I didn't come home at all." A lump formed in her throat. Why did she still *want* her mother to care for her? Wasn't she grown up and self-reliant by now?

Q stroked her leg. "I would notice."

That's because you love me. She doesn't.

"What about your step-father, Robert Klein? He's quite a celebrity. But how is he in real life?"

"He's nice, but we don't have a close relationship."

She didn't say that while Robert was always polite, he'd never talked to her on a personal level. By the way he sometimes looked at her with puppy eyes, she suspected he felt guilty to be the reason her mother had abandoned her way back then.

"I've even been to several of his performances, he truly is a great tenor. His voice is outstanding."

Hilde nodded. "When did you last see him perform?"

"Earlier this year. I saw him sing in *Rheingold* by Richard Wagner and *Iphigenia in Tauris* by Christoph Willibald Gluck."

"You like music?"

"I do. A lot."

"What's your favorite instrument?"

"That's easy. The transverse flute."

Hilde cocked her head. "That's a strange instrument for a man to like."

"Not at all. There is something so soothing about the smooth notes. I should play for you some day."

"I'd love that," Hilde agreed. "I used to like going to the opera and even musical concerts, but since the Nazis have instituted their *Gleichschaltung*, they're destroying even the classic operas. Have you noticed how they changed certain characters and some lyrics in Rheingold to adapt it to the Nazi philosophy?"

"I'm afraid I haven't. It was the first time I've seen this opera." He glanced over to her. "But I'm not surprised. The National Socialism is slowly taking over every aspect of our lives. Whether we want it or not."

"Isn't there something we can do?" she asked, but Q only shook his head and changed the subject. "What about your father?"

"I don't talk to him anymore. Not since I left. He's married to my step-mother, Emma. They have two daughters, my half-sisters, Sophie and Julia."

"How long have you been gone?"

"Four years."

"That's a long time." He reached for her hand to squeeze it before he let it go and grabbed the steering wheel again. "Why did you leave?"

She sighed. *Why?* It had seemed like a good decision, but she wasn't so sure anymore. "We had a fight. I don't even remember the reason. We always fought. My step-mother is the complete opposite of my mother. She was very strict and never let me go out, or do any of the fun things teenagers like to do."

Q chuckled. "You probably fought about something stupid and completely irrelevant for anyone but a teenager. I do remember those days."

Hilde sent him a surprised glance. "I thought you and your mother always got along well?"

"We did. But we still fought when she wouldn't allow me to do things I wanted to do. Isn't that normal?"

Maybe it was, but to her, it had meant a great deal. She'd felt like Emma was out to ruin all her fun, to show her how bad a person Hilde was and how much she disturbed their little family. *How much I wasn't wanted.*

"How old are your sisters?" Q asked.

Hilde had to calculate their ages. "Julia is nine years younger than me and Sophie thirteen. That would make them thirteen and nine by now. It's been such a long time."

"Don't you miss them?"

She crunched her nose. "I'm not sure. See, I was eight years old when my father married Emma and took me to live with them. One year later, Julia was born. I felt so dispensable. I hated her. I envied her for having a mother who cared for her. When Sophie arrived, things got worse. Emma didn't have that much time anymore. She was always occupied with the two little ones and I…" Tears sprang to her eyes.

"*Liebling*, please don't cry. That was a long time ago, and I'm sure she loves you."

"Well, if she did, she hid that part very well," Hilde said stubbornly. "We fought all the time. About everything. And my father always took her side. After one particularly nasty fight, I packed my bags and moved to Berlin to live with my mother."

"Does your mother still talk to your father?"

"Talk? Not that I know of. She hates him with all her heart. I've never heard her say anything nice about him. I guess that's why I haven't spoken to him again. She would make my life hell."

"She may have her reasons," said Q. "We don't know what happened between them and if she still has hurt feelings about their separation."

Hilde snorted. "Hurt feelings? You don't know her. And it was she who left him. He was fighting on the front lines of the Great War when she left him."

"She took you while he was off fighting for his country?" Q asked, unable to hide the surprise in his voice.

"Oh, no. She didn't take me. I was an inconvenience. She dumped me on my grandmother's doorstep and took off with Robert."

"I'm so sorry, *Liebling*. That must have been an awful experience for you."

"It was. My grandmother was the sweetest person around, but I still waited year after year for my mother to come back for me. Or my father."

He grew silent for a few minutes before he asked, "Don't you think it's time to talk to your father and his family again?"

Hilde violently shook her head. "No."

"Hilde, family is important. Don't you want to know if they're doing okay?"

She pressed her lips together. "He knows where I am and hasn't made an effort to contact me. Why should I contact him?"

"It's always difficult to make the first step. Perhaps he's as hurt as you are. Will you at least keep that idea in your head?"

Hilde looked at him and saw the love in his face. Contrary to everyone else in the world, Q indeed cared for her and wanted to help. She gave him credit for his concern, but she wasn't ready to revisit the past and fight her demons. "Fine. But I won't promise anything."

Chapter 22

One year turned into another, and Hilde finally got her chance to meet Q's mother, Ingrid. She lived in Berlin, but up till now, the timing had never worked for Hilde to accompany him to see her.

Hilde had been on edge for days, wanting to make the best possible impression. She stood in front of her closet and eyed her entire wardrobe for hours, choosing an outfit only to discard it the next moment. She heard the clock ticking in the background. *I'm running out of time. If I don't choose something soon, I'll have to go in the nude.* She giggled at the thought. That would definitely make an impression.

Finally, she put on a cream white starched blouse with short sleeves and a tiny vee-neck. The dark green woolen skirt dropped to mid-calf, and she pulled on the matching jacket to finish off her look. She then entered the bathroom to put on some makeup and pinned her shoulder length hair into an elegant roll on top of her head. She glanced into the mirror, satisfied with her efforts. *Exactly the image I want to convey to his mother. She just has to like me!*

Less than a minute later, the doorbell rang, and Q waited for her outside with two flower bouquets in his hands. "For the two women I love," he said and held the bigger one out to her. Hilde's heart melted, and her nervousness was all but gone.

"Thank you so much." She sniffed at the beautiful

orange, yellow, and red flowers and rushed to put the bouquet into a vase before she returned to the door and Q.

They drove more than half an hour until he parked the car in front of a building on the other side of Berlin. The building had definitely seen better days, but that was true for most of the capital.

Q opened the car door for her and helped her out. He pulled a tad harder than necessary, and she flew into his arms. With a mischievous grin, he took the chance to hold her tight for a moment and kiss her neck.

"You did that on purpose," she said once he released her.

"Who? Me? You really think I could do something so unashamed?"

She broke out in laughter and took his hand. Q had the ability to make her feel secure and joyous at the same time. And the more she got to know him, the more she wanted to spend the rest of her life with him.

Q knocked on the door, and a few moments later, an old lady with brilliant white hair and a dark brown skirt and sweater combination opened the door.

"Wilhelm! Come in, come in. And you must be Hildegard." She pulled both of them into the small apartment and hugged first her son and then Hilde.

"Please, just Hilde, *Frau* Quedlin," she said.

"Don't be silly, dear. Call me Ingrid." The older woman released her and glanced her over before turning to Q. "She's beautiful, son."

He winked and nodded. "I know."

Ingrid chuckled and then led the way to the kitchen. "I'm sorry, but this is the only table I have. The place is just too small. Do you want tea?"

"Yes. Please. May I help you with something?" Hilde asked.

"No, dear. My Wilhelm can help. You sit and enjoy." Hilde watched as Q hurried around the small kitchen to do his mother's bidding.

"Hilde, this is such a treat for me. Wilhelm has never brought a girlfriend with him."

Hilde's ears started burning, and she wished she'd worn her hair down. "He hasn't? Well, he shall bring me from now on."

Ingrid smiled at her and reached up to press the cross around her neck between her thumb and forefinger. Hilde's eyes followed the gesture and commented, "That's a beautiful necklace."

"Thank you, dear. It helps me to cope with all the worries and hardships."

Hilde saw the eyes of Q's mother water and she bit her lip. But just a moment later, Ingrid had gathered her composure and asked, "Now, tell me about you, my dear."

"I work at an insurance company."

"That's good. So many people are out of work nowadays. The government does its best to generate jobs, but it's just not enough. They even had to release long-time government employees like my son, Gunther."

Hilde's eyes widened, and Q sent her a warning glare before he nodded. "Yes, it's such a shame he and his family had to move so far away." Turning to Hilde, he added, "Mother is besotted with her grandkids."

Ingrid cocked her head and scrutinized Q as if she was expecting him to add something, but she looked at Hilde again and asked, "Have you met Gunther and his family?"

Hilde dutifully responded, "I met him several months ago, but his wife and sons were absent that day." She didn't add that he hadn't liked her at all – a feeling that was mutual.

"Well, since he's not here, I can tell you Wilhelm was always my favorite son." Ingrid patted his arm and smiled. "Probably because he was born when the others were already half grown. He got all the attention, almost like a single child. I was afraid I spoiled him too much because he never showed interest to marry and have kids."

Q rolled his eyes. "Mother…"

"Come on, Wilhelm. You do have honorable intentions with this lovely girl, don't you?" It was refreshing to notice that, for once, he was the one blushing and squirming. Who'd have thought his mother held that kind of power?

Q turned towards Hilde and said, "Have I told you my mother is a follower of Rudolf Steiner and his theory of anthroposophy?"

Ingrid was quick to explain. "Through meditation, you can control your thinking, your will, and create an atmosphere of impartiality and positivity. It helps to understand the greater picture and calm down your own grief and negativity."

Hilde smiled and nodded, not sure she quite understood. Q must have seen the look of confusion on her face and added, "I like some of Steiner's ideas. Especially his take on organic or biodynamic agriculture. Since I've started working for the Reich Institute, I've studied many of his essays, pointing out the dangers of synthetic fertilizers for the ecosystem as a whole. He promotes the idea that a farm as the smallest agricultural unit thrives through biodiversity, and the integration of livestock and crops into a closed-loop of cross-fertilization."

"Oh, Wilhelm. That's marvelous."

Ingrid's eyes lit up, and Hilde watched as she and her son discussed the benefits and drawbacks of Rudolf Steiner's philosophy. While Q argued from the scientific angle, his mother understood anthroposophy from a more intuitive and spiritual angle.

Both of them had all but forgotten about Hilde, and she sensed a stab to her heart as she witnessed how much love those two held for each other.

Their relationship was so much closer than she'd ever had with her mother or her step-mother. Even when they didn't agree on a point, they never became angry or irritated with the other person.

The more she observed Q's interaction with his mother, the more pensive she became. Since her mother had first left her at the age of two, she'd felt homeless. Unloved. Not even when her father had finally taken her to live with him and his new wife six years later had she felt like she belonged.

Now, in hindsight, she understood Emma was a good woman and had tried to give Hilde a home. But the little girl carried so much hurt with her, she didn't want to accept Emma as a mother. She'd wanted her birth mother to love her!

In fact, her whole life had been a quest for love – to be loved by the one person who wasn't able to give her the love she longed for. At the same time, she'd put up walls around her heart to keep away any other person. Afraid to experience the same rejection and hurt again.

She'd vowed to never love again. To keep her heart safe and sound. Q had been the first person to dig a hole into her wall of defense. He made her feel safe. Loved. The center of his world. She never had any doubts that he might one day abandon her.

"Everything okay?" he asked as they drove back home.

"Just thinking. You have such a good relationship with your mother. Something I never had with either of my parents."

"It doesn't have to be like that. You still have time to reconcile with your father."

She grew quiet, and when they were almost back to their destination, she nodded. "It might be worth trying. Should I write him a letter?"

"A letter sounds like a great first step."

"I'll do it. I'll write the letter tonight and send it off in the morning before work."

Q's eyes showed how proud he was of her. When he dropped her off at her front door, he kissed her lingeringly and said, "I love you."

Her heart stopped. There it was. That dreaded love word. She'd known it all along, since she met him, but today was the first time he'd said it. Her whole body tensed as the meaning of his words settled in her soul. *I love you.* She wanted to repeat those words, but her throat was dry as a sand dune and no words would come out.

As always, Q seemed to know exactly what was going on inside her, because he put a finger to her lips and whispered, "You don't have to say anything, *Hildelein.* I loved you from the first moment I saw you – no, from the first moment I heard you laugh – in the movie theater and every day since then my love for you has grown stronger and deeper." Then he took her tense hands into his and added, "I promise, I will never abandon you. I will love you until I draw my last breath."

Tears pooled in her eyes and she pressed her body against his, embracing him with all her strength, as if she could keep them joined like this forever. And finally – finally – the wall around her heart came crumbling down with a force that almost blew her away. "I love you, too. I love you so much, it almost hurts."

He kissed her cheek and then removed himself from her grip to hold her at arm's length. "Is this why you're weeping?"

She couldn't do anything but nod, and Q wiped away her tears with his finger. "Don't cry, my love."

Hilde kissed him one last time and then slipped inside. She had a letter to write.

Writing the letter was easier than she'd thought it

would be. Maybe it was because the ice that had surrounded her heart for so long had finally thawed.

The next morning, she left for work a few minutes early, sticking the letter into the post box. When she turned around with a feeling of satisfaction and pride, reality knocked in.

A man dressed in nothing but rags shoved a woman waiting at the tram station and ran off with her handbag. Hilde gasped as the woman started screaming, "*Hilfe, ein Dieb!*" pointing to the running man with her handbag.

Within moments, SS policemen were chasing the thief down. He didn't even get two buildings away before he was surrounded. But rather than arresting him, Hilde witnessed how the SS officers began beating him with their wooden bats.

She wanted to puke at the awful spectacle and looked around to see if anyone else had noticed. But all the other passersby continued as if nothing happened; nobody even raised their head to watch. A man was being beaten to death in front of her eyes, and nobody did anything to stop this barbaric behavior. "He's stolen a purse, for god's sake. That's not a capital crime," she murmured to herself.

Her head whirled with emotions, and she took a step forward, driven by the need to stop the horrific scene, only to have her shoulder grabbed harshly. She turned her head and glared into the eyes of a stranger. He dragged her away from the scene, growling at her, "Are you crazy, woman? Do you want to die too? Move along."

Hilde stared at the man, following him like a puppet

around the corner. Only then did he release her, and she came back to reality with a jolt. "Thank you. I was...I'm sorry."

He glanced at her. "Be more careful from now on. It would be a shame. You're such a beautiful young woman."

In a daze, she nodded and turned on her heel to walk to work, not looking at anyone or stopping for anything. But the picture of the SS officers beating a handbag thief to death became deeply ingrained into her mind.

Chapter 23

Q impatiently waited for Hilde to get off work. When she left the building, he waved over and shouted, "Darling, come here. I want to show you something."

Hilde grinned at him. "You're hopping up and down like a small child. Is it already Christmas?"

"No. Better. You'll see."

When they arrived at his place, he said, "Look what I bought."

"A radio? This is the big surprise?" She'd grown accustomed to his excitement about anything technical, but a simple radio?

"It's one of the most technologically advanced radios in existence. A *Volksempfänger*. You know, the one they've been advertising in newspapers and on advertising columns?"

"I've seen the ads," she smiled at him, "but I'm sure there's more to it than meets the eye."

"How did you know?"

Hilde giggled, because after going out more than one year, he still seemed surprised when she knew he was hiding something.

He kissed her and said, "You know me too well. Of course there's more. The little *Goebbelsschnauze* here can only receive middle and long wave, which lets us listen to German stations. I've tinkered with the inner life of our little baby and installed a trap circuit so we can distinguish the weaker signals as well. Wanna listen?"

Q turned the knob, and a French voice sounded from the radio, and they both listened to the broken words. "There's too much interference. This is the problem with middle and long waves. I'll have to think of something better. If I could adapt the *Volksempfänger* to receive short waves as well..."

He had all but forgotten about Hilde and strode over into his office where he searched for a screwdriver on his desk. Hilde followed him and asked, "What are you doing?"

"Here, I found it." He looked up into her confused face. "Sorry, darling, but I just had a great idea. Why don't you make us some coffee, and I'll show you in a few minutes?"

Hilde just rolled her eyes and trotted off. When she came back a while later with two mugs of coffee in her hands, he was sitting at his desk amidst heaps of paper with scribbled sketches, several tools, and wires lying around the brand new radio disassembled into its components. Her voice startled him. "Where should I put the coffee?"

"Coffee? Sure!" He pointed to a corner, and she actually found a spot to set down the mugs. A moment later, she stood at his side and pointed to his desk. "Q, this place is a mess. Let me help you straighten-"

"Don't you touch anything. Everything is right where it belongs."

She glanced around. "There's no way that's true. I

could help you build some files and–"

"No! I like things just like they are. If you straighten it up, I won't be able to find anything."

Hilde rolled her eyes at him again. "I don't know how you find anything now."

He winked at her. "I have my own system. Now, see this." He showed her one of his sketches and explained, "With a smaller reel and copper wires and a few adjustments here and there, our radio can receive short waves."

"And?"

"Hilde, this means we'll be able to hear foreign radio stations as well. Italian operas. French chansons. British history programs. Isn't that great?" *And the real news, not the propaganda our government wants us to believe.*

She put her hands on his shoulders. "Did you see this sticker on the radio? The one that says, 'Hearing foreign radio stations is a crime against national security and will be punished with imprisonment.'"

He stood up and wrapped an arm around her waist. "Don't worry so much. Think of all the possibilities."

Hilde kissed him on the nose. "Please promise me you'll be careful. Don't let anyone know what you're doing."

"Duly noted." He stood and kissed her chin, then her cheek, then the top of her head. He pulled away, not daring to go any further. "And now let's have our coffee. I can finish this tomorrow."

***

In his free time, Q worked relentlessly on several new inventions. One of them was refining the mist filters for gas masks, the same thing he'd researched while still at Auer-Gesellschaft a few years back. It still bothered him a great deal that he hadn't been able to complete that specific task.

He made sure to stay away from the old technology, and finally found a completely different method. A better and cheaper method no less. He tweaked the end results some more to make sure he wouldn't violate any of the patents he'd filed as an employee of the Auer-Gesellschaft.

As soon as he'd filed for and been granted the patent of *Anordnung zur Richtungsbestimmung,* he scouted for companies willing to buy the commercial rights from him. Soon enough, he found a serious prospect.

Drägerwerke was Germany's leading manufacturer of medical equipment, and once he'd sent them a copy of his patent, the head of production had been very anxious to meet with him. A few days later, Q traveled to their headquarters in Lübeck.

During the meeting, it soon became clear why they so badly wanted to buy the commercial rights to his patent. They were after a big military contract from the German government. Apparently, the contract would only be granted if they could provide medical equipment as well as gas masks. And up until now, Auer-Gesellschaft effectively held a monopoly on them, thanks to Q's earlier patents.

Q knew his new method of folding and applying the adhesive was superior to the old one, and that the performance of the gas filters would be greatly enhanced when using it. Drägerwerke was a good company, but Q still had a nagging feeling in his stomach because the head of production was more interested in crushing the competition – Q's former employer – and making big money with the government contract than in providing the cheapest and best possible protection for the general public. Once again, his invention would be used mainly for military purposes.

But when the procurement manager named a staggering figure they were willing to pay for the exclusive commercial rights in Germany, he pushed the nagging feeling away and agreed. After all, he would need a nest egg if he were to marry Hilde and have a family with her, and the amount they offered was equivalent to a three-years' salary.

On his way home, he was disheartened. Why didn't anyone understand his wishes that his inventions should be used for the people and not against them? Why was everyone so keen on Germany's re-militarization? Didn't they see this would inevitably lead to war and complete destruction?

After pondering the situation, he decided not to search for a buyer of the commercial rights for Italy, where he'd already filed for and been granted the patent as well. Any Italian company would only follow the example of Drägerwerke.

Instead, he set up a meeting with his Russian contacts at the Soviet trade mission, confident the communists would use his technology for the protection of the general public and not for profit.

Pavel was surprised to see him after Q hadn't

contacted him in quite a while. "Hello Q, what brings you here?" the agent asked.

"I've been working on improvements for the gas mask filters I showed you earlier."

"Oh, yes, I remember. Your technical knowledge has served our comrades well, but unfortunately, the production process is tedious and cost intensive."

Q nodded. "I know. But my new folding and adhesive technology will solve those problems. I want gas masks to be accessible to every last person in case a new war breaks out."

After some discussion back and forth with Moscow, Pavel produced a very generous offer. "I have good news for you. Your technology is worth quite a lot, and we're very interested in acquiring the commercial rights outside of Germany." He named the exact amount of money Q had already received from Drägerwerke.

Q shook his head. "No. No. I couldn't possibly accept that kind of money. Consider this my contribution to a peaceful coexistence of our nations."

Pavel tried to convince him to take the money, but Q adamantly refused to. Some of his friends probably thought him naïve to pass up so much money, but wasn't it a worthy cause? Giving back to mankind and doing his bit for peace.

He left the Soviet trade mission at Unter den Linden with a whistle on his lips and the feeling of having done the right thing.

Chapter 24

Hilde looked out of the window at her mother's kitchen for the hundredth time. *Why doesn't he come already?* She paced back to the living room, eyeing the letter on the bureau as if it could suddenly spring to life and attack her. Her fingers trembled as she reached for it and touched the soft white paper with her hands. The letter was lightweight and slim, probably only one sheet of paper.

Her name and address were written with a typewriter. No sender. But the postage stamp indicated it came from Hamburg. *It's from my father. It must be.*

She looked at the clock on top of the bureau and then paced back to the kitchen with the letter in hand, looking out of the window once again. *He should be here by now. Why isn't he coming?*

Her first intention had been to tear open the letter in the privacy of her bedroom, but then she couldn't. She'd stood there staring at it, unable to move. What if it contained bad news? If her father didn't want to see her? Or if her mother walked in and caught her opening the letter written by the man she still hated so much? What if Annie destroyed her father's note before she could read the contents? It wasn't safe, Hilde tried to rationalize. She'd wait for Q to arrive. He would know what to do.

She returned to the living room and looked around the place. On the corner of the couch she spied one of her half-brother's *Hitlerjugend* uniforms lying there, together with the ever present swastika arm band and several swastika flags in different sizes. A lump formed in her throat and she had the urgent need to breathe air. Fresh air.

The Nazis had long ago invaded even her most private space. Since her half-brother had joined the NS youth organization, *Hitlerjugend,* there was no escaping the constant propaganda. Not even in the safety of her home. *I have to leave this place. Soon. I feel like I'm drowning.*

With a bitterness that surprised her, she thought that at least on that account her mother shared the same opinion. More than once, she'd told Hilde it was time for her to get married and move out.

Finally, she heard a car approach and saw Q pull up out front. She rushed from the house and climbed into the vehicle, all before he could turn off the engine or even think about coming to get her.

"Happy to see me?" he asked with a wink.

She pulled the envelope from her pocket and thrust it at him. "This came today." Now that he'd finally arrived, the words came tumbling out of her mouth faster than lightning. "It's from Hamburg. It must be from my father, but I was afraid mother would come home and see it, so I hid it in my pocket. I was afraid to open it because I wasn't sure–"

Q chuckled and placed a finger over her lips, effectively silencing her for a moment. "Easy, Hilde. Take a deep breath for me and then start again."

She nodded, swallowing hard. "Can we drive to

your place and open it there?"

"I think I can do that. You don't want Annie to know about the letter?"

"No, I don't. She still hates my father so much. She would disapprove that I contacted him in the first place."

Q drove her to his building and escorted her up the stairs to the little apartment. "Sit down, then open the letter and see what he has to say."

Hilde sat down, and he placed the letter in her lap. She looked around the room, thinking once again how nicely it was decorated considering it belonged to a bachelor. The wooden floors were covered by a large rug, and the couch she sat on had obviously not been used by many people. Two side chairs sat on either side of the couch, stacked high with papers. Q and his penchant to collect everything.

She took a steadying breath and attempted to open the letter, but her fingers were shaking too badly to manage the task.

"Here, let me open it for you." He produced a letter opener and slit the top of the envelope before handing it back to her.

She took a nervous breath and unfolded the paper. The letters sprang around on the paper, but somehow she managed to read the note.

Dear Hilde,

I was so happy to hear from you. All of us have missed you. You are welcome to visit anytime. This is still your home.

Please bring your young man with you. I would love to make his acquaintance.

Love,

Your father

"He sounds happy," Hilde murmured, almost unable to believe her eyes. A huge weight lifted from her chest as she carefully stroked the paper and imagined her father in his office, smoking a cigar while writing the letter.

"Do you want to visit him? I could drive us to Hamburg for a weekend," Q offered.

She nodded, wanting to see her father and yet afraid her happiness would disappear once she got there.

Q produced some paper, a pen, inkwell, and envelope. "Why don't you write him back and give him your phone number as well. That way he can contact you sooner and we can make arrangements to go visit him right away."

She blankly stared at him. "I can't do that. What if he calls and my mother answers the line?"

"True, that could cause a problem." Q furrowed his brow. "Why don't you give him my phone number?"

"You would do that for me?" she asked, lifting the pen up and preparing to start the letter.

He grabbed her around the waist and pressed a kiss to her neck. "I would do anything for you, Hildelein. I love you. Go ahead. Write him with my phone number and then I'll take you out to dinner to celebrate."

"I don't know what to say," Hilde said.

"Then bring that stuff with us and I'll help you write the letter while we wait for our food to arrive. I'm starving."

Hilde smiled and gathered up the writing supplies. Dinner was wonderful, and in no time at all, they had a letter to her father composed.

On the way back to her mother's house, Hilde grew nervous once again. She couldn't purchase a stamp or mail the letter until the morning. Q walked her up to the third floor, but before she could ask him about mailing the letter for her, Annie opened the door. She glanced at them, her eyes locking on the envelope in her daughter's hand.

"What's that? Did the postman leave a piece of mail on the front step?" Annie reached for the envelope, yanking it out of her hands before Hilde could pull it away.

Her mother looked like she'd sucked on a lemon, blatant disgust on her face. "This is for Carl. What on earth do you have to say to your father?"

Q snatched the letter from Annie's fingers and said to Hilde, "I'll mail it in the morning."

"Show me the letter!" Hilde's mother demanded. "I hope you're not complaining about me to this…disgraceful person. Since the day I married him, he's caused nothing but trouble. A man who leaves his wife and baby daughter alone to go sauntering around the world isn't worth the cost of the paper and ink to write him. I refuse to permit you further contact with him."

"Saunter the world? He was a soldier, fighting at the front, for god's sake!" Hilde replied, but her mother only gave her a cold stare.

"Others stayed at home to care for their wives. He chose not to."

"I'll see you tomorrow," Q whispered and kissed Hilde's cheek before he quietly backed out of the corridor and stormed down the stairs as if the devil incarnate was chasing him.

Hilde didn't blame him, knowing another nasty argument with her mother was on its way. She took a steadying breath and attempted to brush past her mother and into the house. If she could reach the safety of her bedroom and close the door before her mother caught up, she might be able to hold onto the happiness she'd felt earlier.

But no such luck. Annie drew level with her a few feet from her room. "You better start looking for another place to stay. In fact, if you insist on having contact with Carl, why don't you go and move back in with him?"

Hilde didn't bother to turn around or respond. She put one foot in front of the other until she reached her room and sank down onto the bed. *I wish I had someplace else to live. I hate this house. I hate her.*

Chapter 25

"Nervous?" Q asked Hilde as they passed the Brandenburger Tor on their way to Hamburg.

"Why would I be nervous? We're only visiting the father I left after a row five years ago and haven't talked to since." She tried a joke but shuddered inwardly. She closed her eyes to take a deep breath. Without Q, she wouldn't be here. He'd nudged her to take the first step and had even offered to accompany her and drive her to Hamburg in his little Ford. Otherwise, she'd have taken the train and probably have jumped at the first stop and run back.

A wave of reassurance washed over her as she observed his slim, long fingers grabbing the steering wheel. He drove the car like he did anything in his life: With meticulous attention to detail and great authority. She loved that man so much, it occupied ever last corner of her body and soul.

Q glanced at her. "Don't overthink it. Everything will be fine."

Hilde nodded and they drove in silence until they reached the new Autobahn to Hamburg.

"With the Autobahn we'll be in Hamburg in no time at all," Q said.

Hilde giggled. "At work that's about everything they talk about. The wonderful new highways, better and faster mobility to everyone. The Nazis should rename themselves to *The Autoparty*."

Q reached out for her hand. "I know. And it may be the only good thing Hitler has done for our country. But then, it's a big show, just like everything else that has happened since the *Machtergreifung*."

Just a few days ago, Berlin had seen another huge deployment of soldiers with colorful parades and thousands of people cheering and celebrating the Führer and his farseeing politics.

"The people are celebrating this man as if he was Jesus Christ personally, God-sent to redeem the German Nation," Hilde said with disgust and turned on the radio, just to hear the newest propaganda by minister Goebbels himself.

"...another great success in the efforts for betterment of our Fatherland. The jobless rate is down from over thirty percent to ten percent in less than three years, since our Führer Adolf Hitler took over..."

She turned off the radio again. "I'll vomit if I have to hear more of this. They claim all the credit for the good things, while they forget to mention how they achieved it." She talked herself into a heated rage. "Do you know why the unemployment rate is dropping so fast? I've seen it with my own eyes. They're firing all the Jews, and taking them out of the statistics. And they've fired many married women who have a working husband. Fine way to decrease unemployment!"

"And don't forget the additional five hundred thousand men they've put into the military," Q added with an amused voice.

Hilde glared at him. "How can you take this so lightly? That's not funny."

"It isn't. But it won't help to get all enraged. On the contrary, it will make us vulnerable. Remember, it's best to keep a low profile? I wouldn't want you to make the acquaintance of a Gestapo officer."

An icy chill traveled down her spine. While nothing official was known, there had been rumors about what kind of things happened during a Gestapo interrogation. Things she didn't even want to imagine, much less experience.

"You're right," she said and fell into silence. "But I still don't get it."

"What don't you get?" Q asked.

"Why the French and British don't mind that Hitler reunified the Saar Basin with the Reich."

"They mind, but they're trying to appease Hitler at this time. They're hoping that by giving him what he wants, he won't ask for more."

"Do you think their strategy will work?"

Q shook his head, "No. I think that decision is going to come back to haunt everyone in Europe and prove to be a huge mistake in years to come."

Hilde lapsed into silence and worried about her own problems. She hadn't seen her father in almost five years. How different would he look? And her sisters?

Her thoughts wandered back in time to the day when he'd returned from the last war and had found his daughter living with his mother while his wife was sharing bed and table with another man. The humiliation and anger on his face had been deeply ingrained into her soul.

Back then, she'd mistaken it for disapproval of herself. And for most of her life she'd encased this hurt, grief, and guilt in her heart. Even though her grandmother had many times explained it wasn't Hilde's fault, she hadn't believed one word that the good woman said. It was her – and only her – fault, that both her mother and her father had abandoned her. She just wasn't worthy to be loved.

Tears sprang to her eyes at the memory. Even when he'd come back from war, she hadn't understood why he'd left her with her grandmother. She loved her grandmother dearly, but she'd longed to live with her parents. Like any five-year-old girl would.

It wasn't until much later that she understood he hadn't been able to care for her and leaving her with his mother had been his only option. There was no way a single man recently returned from the cruelties of war and working all day could take care of a child on his own.

It wasn't until 1920 when her father married Emma that he brought eight-year old Hilde home to live with them. She'd suddenly had a family again, but it wasn't the family she wanted. To give her step-mother credit, the woman had tried her best to be a mother to Hilde. But she'd been hurt and refused to give even a little bit.

Things worsened with the birth of her first half-sister, because the baby reminded her every day that Emma was only her step-mother and her own mother had gotten rid of her.

That was the toughest time she'd faced in her life and she shuddered at the memory. She vowed to never abandon her children, should she be blessed with any.

Hilde sighed, and Q reached over to touch her thigh, "Hildelein, don't worry. Everything will work out."

She turned her head and gave him a smile. "Yes, it will. I love you." *I am so deeply, crazily in love with you, it's almost frightening.* It was a feeling she'd never had before and it consumed every part of her. She wanted to belong to him. She wanted him to be her family and longed to experience the blisses of marriage.

"I love you too." He kissed his forefinger and then tapped it on her lips. "You're going to be just fine. Remember, I'm here with you all the time."

Hilde sighed in relief. Since she had started going with Q, she had become so accustomed to having his reassurance and loving presence in her life. He was her family. Her best friend. Her love. He was everything she could ever have wished for in a man. Q would never hurt her. Or abandon her.

Chapter 26

Q grew increasingly worried about Hilde the farther they traveled from Berlin. Since leaving the city, she'd been unusually quiet and pale. Now, he asked himself if he'd pressured her too much into reconciling with her father and she wasn't emotionally ready.

Her inner turmoil was palpable inside the confinements of his small car, and all he wanted was to make her pain go away. Just how?

When Hilde sighed again, looking out the window, he glanced over and noticed her trembling hands. At the next recreation area, he left the Autobahn.

"Still nervous?" Q asked as he pulled the car to a stop.

A single tear slid down her cheek and he brushed it away with his thumb before he exited the automobile and helped her out. "Come here," he said and embraced her in his arms. They stood still for a long time until he sensed the tension in her body easing.

"Are you okay?" Q asked.

"I guess I am. Just very nervous." Hilde tried a small smile.

"Everything will be fine. If your father was still angry or resentful, he wouldn't have sent such a joyful and welcoming letter."

"I keep telling myself that."

"Well, start believing it."

She laughed. "You make it sound so simple."

He kissed her nose. "It can be, if you'll allow it."

Pulling him close, she listened to his heart under her ear. "How do you always know the right words to say?"

"Because my heart is connected to yours, and it hears what you need."

She melted. Simply melted against him. Yes, she could do this, with him by her side.

After a while, Q led Hilde back into the automobile and started the engine. "Ready to tackle the dragon?"

Hilde giggled. "Well, yes."

Q leaned over for a kiss and said, "That's much better." Then they continued their journey to Hamburg. A short while later, they stopped in front of a modest single family house in the suburbs.

Two teenage girls were sitting on the front porch, rushing into the house before Q and Hilde managed to get out of the car. "Papa. Mama. They're here!"

"Guess someone has been waiting anxiously." Q chuckled.

"Sophie and Julia. They've grown so much."

As soon as Q opened the car door for Hilde, her father appeared in the door. He was a handsome man with greying hair at his temples and bushy grey eyebrows. Q instantly liked the man.

"Hilde, I'm so happy to see you!" He strode towards them, pulled her into his chest and hugged her tight for several long moments. Q could see Hilde's eyes watering and when her father released her, he squeezed her hand in a reassuring gesture.

Hilde made the introductions, "Father, this is Wilhelm Quedlin."

Her father shook Q's hand. "It's a pleasure to meet you, Herr Quedlin."

"Herr Dremmer, the pleasure is all mine, but please call me Q."

Carl Dremmer looked from Q to his daughter and said, "I see. Q it is then. Please come inside."

Her sisters rushed forward to greet them and Q had to hide a grin when they seemed to remember they were supposed to behave and slowed down at the last moment to shake his and Hilde's hand with a curtsy.

Only then did he notice a woman in the background, who'd patiently waited her turn to greet their guests. "Welcome home, Hilde." She stepped forward, smiling away the slight tension he noticed between the two women. Sophie and Julie came to the rescue, cutting the welcome short by grabbing Hilde's hands and pulling her with them back into the house.

"Please excuse the manners of my girls, but they've been anxiously waiting since the day we received Hilde's letter. But you must be hungry, please come in."

Q retrieved their luggage, and soon, the whole family was sitting around the table drinking coffee and eating homemade strawberry cake. After coffee the women disappeared into the kitchen to wash the dishes and prepare dinner.

"Want a drink?" Carl Dremmer asked Q, escorting him into his office.

"Yes, please, Herr Dremmer."

"Nonsense. Please call me Carl."

"Thank you for the warm welcome, Carl."

"No, it's I who should be thanking you for being such a positive influence on my daughter." His voice showed no trace of emotion, but his ticking eyelid revealed how much the man had suffered by being estranged from his oldest daughter.

"You've met my ex-wife?" Carl asked.

Q chuckled. "Yes. She's interesting, to say the least."

Carl made a face. "That's a nice way of saying…well, enough about her. I hope I never have to cope with her again. But please tell me something about you."

The two men chatted for a while until Q cleared his throat. "Since we're alone, there is another reason I wanted Hilde to reconcile with you."

"Oh?" Carl asked, looking interested.

"Yes. I want to ask for your daughter's hand."

"Yes! A thousand times yes," Carl agreed with obvious joy and winked at Q, "under one condition."

Q swallowed hard. "Condition?"

"You have to promise to visit more often."

"I can promise that."

They left the office, Q's heart beating fast at the prospect of a future with Hilde by his side.

Chapter 27

Hilde enjoyed getting to know her sisters again, and when Emma appeared in the doorway, she was humbled by her stepmother's capacity for forgiveness. She hadn't thought it would be so easy to catch up, but it had been, even though she'd hurt Emma a great deal when she was a teenager.

"I can't believe how much the girls have changed," she told Emma as she helped put dinner on the table. So many things had changed in the last five years, but the house was still very much the same.

Her father was beaming from ear to ear when he and Q stepped out of his office and Hilde wondered what those two had talked about. Emma apparently had also noticed his good mood and pulled her aside before everyone sat down to dinner. "Hilde, please don't leave your father again. It nearly broke his heart when you left after the quarrel. He hasn't been the same man since then."

Hilde's eyes filled with tears. Everything had suddenly become too much. "I can't stay, but I can promise to keep in touch and visit more often." She met Emma's eyes. "Thank you for putting up with me and for taking such good care of my father."

Emma hugged her. "You're very welcome."

"I'm sorry I was such a brat."

"You were a hurting teenager. But let's not talk about the past."

Hilde laughed, feeling her heart ease even more, and they joined the rest of the family in the dining room. Later that night, Q was assigned Julia's room while Hilde joined her sisters in Sophie's room. The three girls giggled and chatted until very late that night and Hilde felt as if she was on a sleepover with her girlfriends. Except that her younger sisters peppered her with questions about Berlin and her life in the capital.

"What's the city like?" Julia asked, her eyes bright with excitement.

"Are there lots of cute boys?" Sophie chimed in.

"What do you know about boys?" Hilde asked with a chuckle and tried to recall what she'd been like at this age. She felt sure boys hadn't even been on her mind.

"Tell us what it's like," they begged.

"Well, the city is big. There are movie theaters and the opera. Concerts and parades."

"That sounds so exciting. Can we come visit you?"

Hilde started to give an immediate "yes" but paused before saying more cautiously, "I'll speak with Father about it. Maybe you could all come for a visit?"

Much later, when her sisters had fallen asleep, she lay awake. The girls were young and naturally assumed that everything was bigger and more exciting in the capital. She'd thought the same thing at their age, but in reality, her life was rather normal.

Work. Going out with Q. Movies or the theater. Once in a while a trip to the Baltic Sea. Those were the most exciting things she could think of.

The next day, Hilde's heart warmed at the way Q interacted with her youngest sister, Sophie. They were becoming best friends. When Sophie came running over to her, Hilde smiled, "You and Wilhelm are getting along."

"Wilhelm?" She wrinkled her nose. "He said I could call him Q."

"That's what all of his friends call him."

"You're so lucky, Hilde. He's so handsome and intelligent, and he has an answer to all of my questions."

"Don't be a bother, okay?" Hilde warned her, worried Q might become annoyed with all of her questions.

"Your sister is so cute and very curious," Q told Hilde a while later.

"She informed me you are very intelligent." Hilde grinned.

Q chuckled. "It's not hard to appear intelligent to an eleven-year old. But she's so interested in everything going on, I have to keep reminding myself not to say anything political. She's much too young to be involved with those things."

"I agree. Thank you for watching out for her." She slung an arm around his waist. "She should have a carefree childhood and not be bothered with those things."

Later that day, she and Q were talking with her parents about the changes the Nazis had made to the education system. "It's not really about learning anymore. The education nowadays consists mainly of drilling in the National Socialist philosophy. And they added a new subject. *Rassenkunde*."

"Ethnogency? As in theory of the races?" Q asked with raised eyebrows. "In school?"

Carl nodded. "Yes. They come home with all kinds of bullshit ideas planted in their heads. And I can't do anything about it. I can't complain or correct them, because if they were to say the wrong thing to their teacher, they would get in trouble."

Emma sent her husband a stern look. "It is as it is. We should be grateful they are such good girls."

"I'm still worried about them. Since Julia has joined the *Bund Deutscher Mädel*, which is Hitler's version of a girl's club, she's talking all the time about how important sports are to prepare young men and women for war. At least Sophie is too young, so I've been able to keep her out of the BDM for at least another year."

Hilde swallowed and pressed her fingertips to her temples. "They're preparing the kids for war?"

"All signs are pointing to war," Q confirmed.

Carl made a face as if he'd swallowed a lemon. "I'm afraid sooner rather than later. Thank God, I'm too old for that. My experiences in the last war are more than enough for a lifetime."

Emma interrupted the discussion. "The girls should be home any minute. Have you heard Sophie sing?"

Carl beamed with pride. "She's very talented and has a great voice."

"Father, Q plays the transverse flute. Doesn't Sophie have one as well? Maybe the two of them could play some music for us?"

"That's a wonderful idea. Q, do you mind?"

"Not at all." Q headed indoors to find the flute and his musical partner, who had just arrived home. Fifteen minutes later, Q and Sophie were making beautiful music together while the rest of the family listened.

Hilde fell more in love with him as each moment passed. *My father likes him. Emma and my sisters like him. Even my mother likes him, even though her reasons have nothing to do with his character and everything with his material worth.*

The weekend passed far too quickly, and soon, she and Q were headed back to Berlin. In the car, they recounted the past two days, laughing over her sister's antics. Q squeezed her hand. "Hilde, I really liked your family. From now on we should visit them more often."

"Yes, we should do that. This weekend was fun."

Q was silent for a few minutes and then spoke, "I enjoyed getting to know your father, and I asked him for your hand in marriage when we were in his office the day we arrived. He said yes, so I was wondering if you would marry me?"

Hilde's eyes widened as she looked at him and then laughed. Q had just asked her to marry him in the most un-romantic way she could imagine. But this was him. Practical. Result-oriented. She wasn't surprised at all, or disappointed that he had proposed to her while driving his automobile.

She squeezed his thigh. "Yes."

Q smiled at her and said, "We can start making plans as soon as we get back to Berlin. First of all, we need to find a flat that is big enough for both of us."

"That sounds wonderful. What about our honeymoon?" she joked, but Q furrowed his brows and answered, absolutely serious.

"I've thought about that, too. What do you think, if we take a sabbatical to travel across Europe? Three months shouldn't be a problem. I've saved some money and you could ask for unpaid vacation-"

"Q, don't you think we should actually get married first?" She laughed at him.

He glanced over at her. "If you insist. But I've never been happier. I want to live life to the fullest with you. The sooner, the better. You never know how long it will last."

Chapter 28

Life picked right back up and Hilde and Q started making a list of the things they needed to do before they could get married. Find an apartment. Apply for a marriage license. Organize the reception. Prepare for the honeymoon.

Even after they settled for a date, the list continued to grow, but their need to relax didn't.

It was increasingly difficult to find fun things to do because the National Socialists had usurped every last part of German day-to-day life. Even the first ever color movie, *Becky Sharp,* which Q invited Hilde to watch, was embedded with short propaganda films.

Which reminded Q that he'd not given his Russian contact any information lately. But now, with more than himself at stake, Q didn't dare to visit the Soviet trade mission again. Instead, he sent Pavel a note and from then on, they met regularly at ever changing public places. The Berlin Zoo park, the Wannsee Lake, an art exhibition.

About one month after his proposal, Hilde waived a piece of paper at him when he arrived to pick her up. "You won't believe what this is?" she said with a sour face.

"Don't I at least get a kiss?" he asked.

She gave him a half-hearted kiss before she blurted with a high-pitched voice, "The Reichstag has passed another racial law."

"Let me see," he said and took the paper from her shaking hands. According to the piece of paper, all couples eager to marry must now abide to the *Law for the Protection of German Blood and German Honor* that forbade marriages and extramarital intercourse between Jews and Germans. "Neither of us is Jewish, so this won't hinder us from getting married."

Hilde pierced him with angry eyes. "You haven't heard all of it. You now have to prove you're Aryan to get permission to marry. The man at the civil registry explained that we both have to present a *Lesser Aryan Certificate.*"

Looking into her worried eyes, it dawned on him that this might mean a delay for their wedding plans. He sighed. "What do we need to get this certificate?"

She shoved another paper into his hand that indicated the requirements. "Here."

The document explained that seven birth or baptism certificates were required – the person wanting to get married, his parents, as well as maternal and paternal grandparents. Additionally, three marriage certificates, one for each set of parents and grandparents. In lieu of the original documents, they could submit certified proofs.

"Oh my, we better start gathering the documents right away." He sighed and reached out to embrace her. "Don't worry."

She pressed her cheek against his chest. "We can't apply for the license and fix a date before we have the required certificate. And the man at the civil registry warned me that there is already a long waiting time, because since the law was passed a few days ago, no more weddings have been scheduled."

Hilde's father and her mother helped gather the needed documents, and as 1936 arrived, she held her Lesser Aryan Certificate in her hands. But they faced unforeseen problems on Q's side.

His maternal grandmother had been born in Temesvar, Hungary and thus was suspected to be non-Aryan by descent. After several letters back and forth to the authorities in Temesvar, it became clear that they couldn't produce a birth certificate of Q's grandmother. Despite his mistrust for Hilde, Q's brother Gunther offered to help and send an official letter in his position as lawyer.

***

Many a time Hilde confided in her friends Erika and Gertrud that she was beginning to lose hope of ever getting married. Every time they got close to fixing a date, they were forced to postpone it. Again and again and again.

On one occasion, she told her friends, "I'm so fed up with all of this, I'm going to cancel the wedding and break up with Q."

Gertrud laughed at her. "As if you could do that, Hilde. You love that man so much."

Hilde dropped her face into her hands. "It's true. If I didn't know he's the one, I would have given up on the idea of marriage months ago. I hate those stupid racial laws and what they make us go through."

Gertrud padded her arm. "I agree. They're a pain,

and we sure could do without them."

"Don't say that," Erika chimed in. "Those racial laws may be inconvenient at times, but they do serve a purpose. We may not understand them, but the people who made them are much wiser than we are."

Hilde and Gertrud exchanged eye rolls behind Erika's back but let their friend continue to sing the praise of racial segregation.

By mid-year, as they were still attempting to prove Q's Aryan heritage, it became hard to ignore the signs of a totally different kind of trouble. Germany was preparing for war. The neighboring European countries were preparing for war. Even the Russians were preparing for war.

"England is preparing for war," Q told Hilde one evening after listening to BBC radio on his enhanced *Volksempfänger*.

She nodded. "You said this day was coming. Isn't there anything that can be done to prevent it?"

"I'm afraid not. And there's more troubling news. I heard they're building a new super-prison in Oranienburg. Apparently, it will be at the same location currently housing a small concentration camp for political prisoners."

"How do you know all of this?" She snuggled up to him.

He tapped her nose. "Oranienburg is a small place. When I lived there, I knew some of the guards. Most of them have been replaced by SS men because they haven't been strict enough with the prisoners."

Hilde shuddered and didn't ask what *strict* meant. If

it was anything similar to the rumors she'd heard about the way suspects were treated at the Gestapo headquarters in Prinz-Albrecht-Strasse, then she didn't want to know.

Q continued, "Apparently all persons considered a political danger to the Nazi regime can end up there without judicial review or the right to a lawyer. Communists, social democrats, critics, and everyone who dares raise his voice against the Nazi system. Well those, and everyone who's deemed undesirable, including the homeless, beggars, criminals, homosexuals and even Jehovah's Witnesses."

"Oh my God, that's basically everyone! You say one wrong word and you end up in one of those camps? That can't be true."

"I'm afraid it is." Q pressed Hilde against his body and kissed her. "This is why you have to be careful. Don't ever criticize the government."

Hilde's palms broke out into a cold sweat and she turned uncomfortably in his arms, "I didn't tell you…"

His brows furrowed. "Didn't tell me what?"

"The day I mailed my father that first letter, there was this man. He stole a woman's purse. She started screaming and SS officers came from everywhere. They caught up with him and beat him to death in the street."

She swallowed, knowing he wouldn't like the next part. "I was so upset, I wasn't thinking straight. I took a small step forward, trying to keep them from killing him, but some stranger grabbed my shoulder, pulled me away, and lectured me."

Q hugged her close, a long sigh of relief exiting his lungs. "Thank God he did. They probably would've killed you too. Please promise to be more careful."

"I promise, but I can't get the picture of that man out of my head."

He kissed her hair. "It will remind you to be careful."

***

Eight months after Q's proposal, Hilde had almost lost all hope. "We'll never be able to get married," she sobbed into his shoulder.

"Hilde, sweetheart. I love you so much. What difference does a wedding certificate make?"

She looked at him with questions in her eyes, and he continued, "I don't care whether or not we're officially married, we could still live together."

"But that would be very unusual and inappropriate."

"I know," Q said against her lips. "But what other choice do we have? I hate seeing you so upset by all of this."

"I'll be fine. Maybe we should even travel to Temesvar to take things into our hands?"

Q hugged her tight. "That's my girl. And if Gunther's last letter to the former priest in Temesvar doesn't produce anything, we'll do just that."

A knock on the door startled them, and Hilde wondered who it could be. An unexpected knock on the door was almost never a good thing. Q opened the door and Hilde saw his curious neighbor peering into the flat.

"Doctor Quedlin, the postman left this registered letter earlier in the afternoon."

Q took the letter from her hand, and when he didn't offer an explanation, the neighbor added, "It's from Hungary. Does it contain documents pertaining to your marriage?"

Hilde saw the amused smile on Q's face as he answered the woman, "Thank you very much for accepting the letter and taking the trouble to bring it over."

The eyes of the neighbor were glued to the letter. "Don't you want to open it?"

"I sure do. I'll need to go to my office for the letter opener. Thank you so much again." With these words, he closed the door and Hilde grinned from ear to ear.

"That woman sure is nosy. Now let's see what it says."

"Hm. I believe someone else is nosy too," he teased.

"Come on, we've been waiting such a long time. Open it before I tear it apart."

"But only because it's you asking." Q fetched the letter opener and Hilde's heart stood still while he fingered a document from the envelope. "A baptism certificate from the Catholic Church in Temesvar." He dropped the document onto the table and spun Hilde around. "We can get married now."

"Finally," she cried, holding onto him with all her

strength. "I almost stopped believing it would ever happen."

He kissed her hard. "I'll apply for the Aryan certificate first thing tomorrow morning."

Chapter 29

The next day, when Q picked her up at work, he had to report yet another obstacle. "I'm sorry, sweetheart, but the official at the wedding bureau informed me that in addition to the Aryan certificate, we now need a health certificate as well."

"A health certificate? Why that?" Hilde frowned.

"Apparently, another law was passed a while ago, the Marital Health Law. It requires all engaged couples to present a recent medical document proving they are free of a long list of hereditary diseases. This is supposed to keep the German race 'clean and healthy.'"

Hilde stomped her foot. "All of these stupid laws! When will they end?"

"I don't know. I agree they're ridiculous, but there's nothing we can do. Except maybe run away and get married in some other country."

She cocked her head. "That sounds like a good idea, and if there's anything else they require us to do, we should contemplate that option."

Q took his hand in hers. "But then you can't have the reception we've planned with all our friends and family celebrating with us."

She pouted. "Okay, we'll go to the doctor and get that damn certificate. Compared to compiling the paperwork, it sounds easy."

While they waited for the blood samples to be

analyzed and the certificate mailed to them, life continued as usual.

Q worked on new inventions in his free time, always with the goal to protect lives in an upcoming war. One of his best ideas was the improvement on the existing echo-sound system that would work for both ships and airplanes. He even offered the commercial rights to the United Kingdom Admiralty, but they were satisfied with their current systems.

The Royal Air Force, though, was very interested in a workable echo-sound for their airplanes and asked him to deliver a working prototype, not just theories on paper. This unfortunately proved to be impossible because Q didn't have the means to produce a prototype on his own. Plus, if the German authorities ever found out, they'd confiscate his work and declare them, "war important property of the Reich."

He continued to meet with the Russian agent and gave all of his knowledge away for free to Russia. It humored him that he could sell one and the same thing to the rich and give for free to the poor. One day, an intermediary even connected him to the United States War Ministry, who were very interested in some of Q's inventions. Apart from an extensive questionnaire, nothing ever came out of it.

Exactly one year after the day Q proposed to Hilde, both of them received their health certificates in the mail. But when they finally held their marriage license in hand, it was late July 1936 and all of Berlin was in a flurry of activities to host the Summer Olympic Games. There was no way they could get married and have a reception until after the games.

Everything in the capital revolved around the upcoming Olympics. Last minute work was done on the new track and field stadium, the gymnasiums, and other arenas. To help assuage the IOC's concerns over the anti-Semitism prevalent in Nazi Germany, Hitler added a token participant with a Jewish father to the German team. The Nazis even "cleaned up" the entire city of Berlin in preparation for the arrival of the world.

Q watched with wonder as the city of Berlin changed before his eyes. The party removed signs stating "Jews not wanted" from the city and the main tourist attractions. All beggars, invalids, street kids and, Romany gypsies were removed from the city and contained in a special camp during the Olympic Games.

But what struck Q most were the non-obvious changes. People seemed friendlier and all of a sudden the oppressive, bleak atmosphere gave way to a tolerant, friendly, and cosmopolitan one, the way Berlin had been a decade ago. Everyone smiled and people went out of their way to help the arriving foreign tourists and athletes.

The Nazi propaganda newspaper *Der Stürmer* was ordered to be sold below the counter. The visitors shouldn't witness any visible evidence of the everyday cruelties.

When walking around the center, Q got the impression things in Berlin weren't all that bad. Was Hitler changing for the better? Would things finally normalize? Q was willing to give the government the benefit of a doubt.

When the big day of the opening ceremony came, Q

surprised Hilde with tickets to witness this spectacular event. Apart from the thousands of people filling the stadium, the eyes of the entire world lay on Berlin because the games were broadcast on television for the first time.

For weeks, everyone had been talking about the historic Olympic Torch Relay and how everyone would always remember the games held in Berlin because it was the first time the torch was relayed all the way from Olympia in Greece to the Olympic Village in Berlin.

"Here he comes," Q said to Hilde over the roar of the crowd when the last torch bearer ran out of the tunnel and into the stadium. Hitler himself was seated in his special box that overshadowed everyone else's, gracefully accepting the cheers and screams of the crowd begging him to step out and show himself to the masses.

But the moment Fritz Schilgen entered the stadium and carried the torch up the stairs to the cauldron, all eyes followed the torch in his hand until he lit the eternal Olympic Flame.

The organizing committee around *Reichssportführer* Hans von Tschammer had pulled all the stops to choreograph a glorious ceremony and had arranged for twenty-five thousand pigeons to be released just after the cauldron was lit. Like everyone else, Q felt the enchantment of the white pigeons flying high in the sky and put his arm around Hilde's shoulders.

Peace doves. Maybe that's a sign to the rest of Europe that Hitler is willing to negotiate in peace.

But the beautiful spectacle ended the moment the

cannon was shot off. The sound literally scared the poop out of the pigeons, and Q could hear the pitter patter of pigeon poop landing on the spectators all around him. He turned to look at Hilde, whose straw hat was specked with rather unpleasant droppings.

She grinned at him from beneath the brim of her hat, her nose wrinkled up as she helped wipe the pigeon poop from his hair.

"Thank you," he said after the nasty business was complete.

"No problem. I wonder who came up with the idea of the pigeons?"

"I wonder if they're still walking around freely?" Q added.

"Let's hope they are. I'm looking forward to watching the competitions. The entire city feels different."

Q agreed. "Let's hope it continues."

But their hopes became thinner as the games wore on. The black US American athlete, Jesse Owens, soon became the darling of the public and the crowd never missed an opportunity to cheer him on. Owens could have been the perfect hero of the games, winning four gold medals, if it wasn't for Hitler's refusal to congratulate him at each medal ceremony.

Hilde and Q witnessed more than one otherwise true-to-party-lines Nazi criticizing the Führer for his refusal to acknowledge Owens' outstanding achievement. After Owen won the one-hundred-meter race, Hitler stood up, tossed his chair back, and rushed from the stadium in a fit of fury.

Q almost couldn't believe his eyes. Not only were one hundred thousand visitors in the stadium privy to a glimpse of the real Hitler, but the whole world on television were witnesses as well. "This is the end of Berlin's Midsummer Night's Dream."

And the following weeks proved him correct. After the tourists left and the television cameras were turned off, terror and despotism took over. Nazi Germany was back in full force, bigger and badder than before the games. And the German people had nowhere to go for help. The world had been at their door, but the image they had taken away was only a mirage, hiding true evil inside.

Chapter 30

Once the dust had settled, Q and Hilde made quick plans to get married. They were both fed up with making wedding preparations only to have to cancel them and decided on a clandestine wedding.

"I don't want to jinx it and make a bunch of plans again," Hilde said.

"Then we won't."

"I'm afraid if we wait too long, someone will pass another stupid law or somehow sabotage our wedding another way. I just want to be your wife."

Q grinned. He'd never been the advocate for a big wedding, but he'd agreed because Hilde wanted it. "Your wish is my command. We'll take the earliest date available at the registry office and won't tell anyone about it. Just you and me."

But the closer the date came, the more he grew quiet and withdrawn. Hilde had asked him several times if he was nervous, and each time, he nodded and changed the topic. Because the truth was, he felt guilty. He was torn…between his love for her and his need to protect her.

In the two years they'd been together, Q had never once mentioned his "other" activities, because he thought the less she knew, the better it was for her. He had become overly careful in his intelligence work, but if he were found out, he'd be hauled away without a trace. And Hilde would have no idea what had happened. She might even believe he abandoned her.

The thought tore him apart. His deception was tearing him apart. The lying had to stop. He couldn't base his marriage on a lie.

Two days before the settled date, he decided to come clean with her and said, "Hilde, let's go for a walk."

She nodded and he took her hand, walking with her until they reached the park. "Q, what's wrong?" she said, her face a mask of fear and uncertainty.

God help me. I hope I'm doing the right thing.

"I need to tell you something. Please, listen to all of it, and then, if you don't want to marry me, I'll understand. But I love you so much, I cannot base our marriage on a lie."

The panic on her face sent shockwaves of pain through his body and he hurried to explain himself.

"I've been secretly working with the Russians by giving them technical knowledge and gathering intelligence for the last several years."

***

"What did you just say?" Hilde's veins filled with ice. As he repeated the statement, she studied his handsome face, and suddenly, his behavior over the last weeks made sense. She'd suspected there was more to his unusual withdrawal than nerves, but never in her wildest imagination had she imagined he was actively working against the Hitler regime.

"Q...I, what?"

"Hilde, I didn't want to tell you. I thought I was protecting you, but then I realized I had to trust you enough to tell you my biggest secret."

Hilde looked at him, but instead of the tall, thin man she'd fallen in love with, she now saw him being hauled off by the Gestapo. Tortured. Humiliated. Locked away in one of the camps for political prisoners. A place where no one returned.

Her eyes filled with tears. "Why?"

"I had to do something. This was my way of fighting back. At first, I thought I could help prevent war, but now I just hope to make it as short as possible."

"You know what will happen…"

Q squeezed her hands. "I do know. It's a risk I'm willing to take, but not one I expect you to shoulder without having time to consider it." He released her hands and stepped back. "I understand if you want to break our engagement. It would break my heart, but I love you so much, I don't want to put you in danger."

"Q…"

He looked deeply into her eyes and she could see all his love for her, and deep down, she saw the unrelenting spirit, the drive to do the right thing. That was why she'd fallen in love with him, but would she be able to withstand the constant threat? Could she be as unrelenting as he was?

Q watched her closely. "Hildelein, if you want me to, I could stop my scouting work. For you."

A million thoughts and feelings attacked her mind and body. The minutes passed and she still wasn't able to form a coherent thought. "My love, I need to sleep on this. It's too much to take in right now."

He nodded. "I understand. Let me take you home."

Hilde stopped him. "Q, I love you, I really do, but I need to be alone right now." She kissed him goodbye and walked away without looking back.

Hilde tossed and turned most of the night, knowing he'd expect an answer the next day. Her love for this man was overwhelming, more than she'd thought she was capable of. But what he was doing was dangerous. And not just to him. If she married him, the Gestapo would never believe she wasn't at least passively involved in his illegal activities.

Should she still marry him or not? Was he worth risking her life for? As she headed to work the next morning, she still didn't know the answer.

Chapter 31

After Hilde left, Q wandered aimlessly through the park. The leaves on the trees had turned into the most beautiful shades of yellow, orange, and red. The last rays of sunshine bathed the landscape in a golden glow, but he couldn't enjoy this beautiful October day.

He'd dropped a bomb on his beloved Hilde by telling her his secret, and now all he could do was wait for her to make the most difficult decision in her life. *Alea iacta est.* The die is cast. Now it was her turn and there was nothing he could do about it. Her decision might break his heart or change the course of his life.

A few hours later, his mind was still in turmoil. On one hand, he felt relieved that she knew the truth and he didn't have to lie anymore, but on the other hand, his words had caused Hilde so much pain. Even though the image of the agony in her eyes when he'd come clean about his subversive activities haunted his mind, he would do it all again.

He loved Hilde so much, and if she decided she couldn't go through with their wedding now that she knew, he would understand. It would break his heart, but he would understand. The image a future without Hilde in his life made him groan, but that wasn't his choice to make.

With nothing else to do than wait, he returned home, but didn't manage to stay there for long before he walked out again into the clear and cold October night.

An exact half-moon rose to the sky and dampened the shine of the stars. The golden moonlight shone bright and clear onto the quiet capital while he wandered around most of the night, thinking about what was important in his life.

The answer to that question had changed over the last few years. Before meeting Hilde, it was his personal mission to try and prevent the war from occurring. But Hilde had taken up so much space in his heart and his life that his priorities had changed. He had to keep the love of his life safe. Even if that meant protecting her from himself.

As he passed an immense chestnut tree – the chestnuts already fallen to the ground and the leaves about to follow them soon – his mind recognized the inevitable end to all life. *Why am I living in this place and at this time? Why not thirty years ago? Or thirty years in the future? What is the reason of my being? What will be my legacy?*

Questions only time could answer. Time that was moving all too slowly today.

When the sun rose over the morning mist, he finally went home and climbed into his bed. In the afternoon, he headed to the insurance office, anxious to see Hilde and find out her decision.

When she came out and walked toward him, his heart jumped with joy only to miss a beat the next moment when he noticed a furrow between her brows.

Hilde greeted him with the same full-blown smile and passionate kiss as always, which he took as a good sign.

"Feel like taking a walk?" he asked.

"Yes. Let's go to the Zoo," Hilde suggested and he grinned. The immense Berlin Zoo park had become one of their favorite places in the city to hang out and relax.

Q clasped her hand in his own. The park was only a few blocks away and soon they were strolling under chestnut and linden trees. She eventually pulled him to a stop, glancing around to make sure they didn't have unwelcome listeners.

"Hilde…"

"Q…"

They both chuckled at having spoken at the same time. She bit her lip and tried again, and it took all of his self-control to stay quiet and listen.

"Yesterday, what you told me was shocking. Not because I don't approve you doing those things but because I could only see the potential threat." She raised a hand and cupped his cheek. "It was a difficult decision and I'm well aware of the implications, even for my own life. But try as I might, I cannot get around the fact that I love you and don't want to live one minute of my life without you."

Q waited, holding his breath as she tried to finish. "And I do want you to continue fighting the Hitler regime, because it's the right thing to do and I'm actually proud of you."

She smiled at him and relief flooded his system.

"We will marry tomorrow," she continued," and stay together until death do us part. Come hell or high water. The rest we'll figure out. Together."

Q was so relieved, deliriously happy and stunned into a momentary silence. When that moment passed, he swept her up into his arms and kissed her passionately. He swirled her around, lifting her up, and making her giggle in response.

"You've just made me the happiest man in the world," he said, setting her back onto her feet and kissing her once more.

Hilde looked at him with love shining in her eyes, "I love you, Wilhelm Quedlin."

"And I love you, Hilde Dremmer. I promise to always love you, no matter what."

Hilde leaned up on her tiptoes and kissed his lips. "So, are you ready to get married tomorrow?"

Q nodded. By tomorrow at this time, they would be Mr. and Mrs. Wilhelm Quedlin. They were finally getting married and all his dreams would come true.

Hilde and Q still have a long journey to go during this war. Book 2 will be released around autumn 2016.

Thank you for taking the time to read UNRELENTING. If you enjoyed it, please consider telling your friends or posting a short review. Word of mouth is an author's best friend.

Thank you,

Marion Kummerow

Acknowledgements

Writing this book was a long and rewarding journey, and I couldn't have done it without help. First of all I want to thank my terrific cover designer Daniela from **www.stunningbookcovers.com**. She has made a wonderful cover for me, while putting up with my endless change requests and a process that took more than a month to finalize the cover.

Then I want to thank my awesome editor Lynette, who was the first person to read the rough outline of this novel and who loved it from the first moment. Without her encouragement I might have abandoned the unfinished work.

Thanks to A.Z. Foreman of **http://poemsintranslation.blogspot.de/** for allowing me to use his translation of the poem of Lorelei:

The fairest of maidens is sitting

So marvelous up there,

Her golden jewels are shining,

She's combing her golden hair.

She combs with a comb also golden,

And sings a song as well

Whose melody binds a wondrous

And overpowering spell.

In his little boat, the boatman
Is seized with a savage woe,
He'd rather look up at the mountain
Than down at the rocks below.

I think that the waves will devour
The boatman and boat as one;
And this by her song's sheer power
Fair Lorelei has done.

Contact Me

I truly appreciate you taking the time to read (and enjoy) my books. And I'd be thrilled to hear from you!

If you'd like to get in touch with me you can do so via

Twitter:

http://twitter.com/MarionKummerow

Facebook:

http://www.facebook.com/AutorinKummerow

Website

http://www.kummerow.info

19999797R00125

Printed in Poland
by Amazon Fulfillment
Poland Sp. z o.o., Wrocław